IMAGINARY MINDS

By

Marlene Lewis

PublishAmerica
Baltimore

First printing

Hardcover 978-1-4512-9146-9
Softcover 978-1-4489-4164-3
PAperback 978-1-4512-6721-1
PUBLISHED BY PUBLISHAMERICA, LLLP
www.publishamerica.com
Baltimore

Printed in the United States of America

Special thanks to my siblings for all the ideas as we were growing up, and my husband, David, for different inspirations that I added to the book.

Highland Academy was based on the school my mother attended in Olivet, Illinois, Vermilion Grove Academy.

Contents

I. The Wedding

Sarah Linzee was running around in a scurry. Her sisters were helping her as much as they could. She motioned for her older sister. "Paula, will you zip my dress?" she asked. She walked over to her younger sister, Nina, "How does my make up look?" Nina responded with great expression, "You look very pretty!" Her blue crepe dress looked beautiful with her dark brown eyes. Today was Sarah's wedding day. She was so excited to be "Mrs. Seth Wiley".

"Mom, can I wear your pearl earrings and necklace? Remember something borrowed, something new, and something blue. I will have all three," Sarah suggested. "Her mother, Hannah, replied, "Of course, Sarah, you can borrow my beads. Just don't forget to give them back."

As Hannah went to the antique wooden jewelry box of her grandmothers and grabbed the pearl earrings and necklace, she said, "These pearls were a birthday gift to me from your dad. He told me he had a surprise for me, handed me the pearl earrings and necklace and said, "I love you with all my heart. I want to spend the rest of my life with you." He then pulled the wedding ring out of his pocket. He said, "Will you marry me?" Special pearls, they are, and now you know why," Hannah responded as she held them close to her chest.

Of course, Seth Wiley was just as stunning. He had purchased a new navy suit with a light blue shirt. His brilliant blue eyes blend just right with the shirt. His teeth were sparkling white which made his gorgeous smile. He also donned a new fedora hat. His black dress shoes were polished to a lustrous shine. He was ready for this special day. Seth was a handsome young man whom everyone liked.

Seth looked at his dad and said, "You know, dad, I am the luckiest man in the world, getting a woman like Sarah for a wife." Noah looked at his son and spoke, "Remember to treat her special all your life. Did I ever tell you the story of how your great grandpa tried to get on the good side of his in-laws? They were all outside one evening and a big old buzzard landed on a tree about one-half mile away. Your great grandpa John said, "I can hit that old buzzard with my rifle, a 22 lever action." This buzzard had landed on an old oak snag tree. This tree was the only tree in the middle of the field. He aimed and that old buzzard dropped dead. His father-in-law never did cuss. He said, "Darn, by golly, you did hit that bird! That just had to be a lucky shot!" From then on old grandpa John was in good with his in-laws. "Ha! Ha!" Noah chuckled, and he just kept on laughing a deep laugh.

Hannah, Paula, and Nina worked on the preparations for the wedding. Hannah had stitched little nylon bags. The girls were busy placing rice in these little nylon bags, and placing a pink and blue ribbon around each one. The rice bags were to be handed to the guests as they entered the church.

Paula had prepared a book for the guest registration. She purchased a scrap book from the five and ten store, and added a few wedding cutouts she had designed. She neatly decorated the front with a picture of Seth and Sarah sitting in the old Model A of Seth's father. Seth and Sarah had went on many a date in this vehicle. Hannah had taken a photo of the both of them as they were in the car getting ready to head for church.

Hannah made the wedding cake from scratch. She let the cake cool. She then mixed up the powdered sugar icing, and as she was icing the cake, motioned with her hand, "Look, Nina, How does the icing look? I added some blue dye for the trimmings and placed on the white icing. How do you like the blue roses I made? That took a lot of practice. Good idea, don't you think?" Hannah questioned. "The roses look great, mom. Wow! How did you make the roses," Nina responded. "I just kept practicing and after about ten roses I finally got the hang of it. I feel like I am an expert now," Hannah said.

Nina was ironing their clothes and polishing the shoes. Shopping from the catalog for new outfits had been so much fun. Removing the tags and pressing the clothes, Nina admired each outfit. "We did a good job choosing our outfits, didn't we, mom?" Nina asked. "You sure did," Hannah responded, "and some good prices, too."

At the church the men were donning the car with a string of cans and "Just Married" signs. Lyle spoke, "Let's put a string of cans on both sides. We'll follow them and drive down town Covey and wake the whole town up. We'll have so much noise, the town and country people will wonder what's happening."

Sarah and Seth wanted just a small simple wedding. Family and friends gathered at the small country church a few miles from the Wiley's home. Seth's family had attended this church for several generations. Seth had sung many specials as a lad, and when he was older, he volunteered for the (very much needed) song leader position. With a very distinguished voice, he could be heard leading the congregation with every song.

The wedding began as Tiera, Seth's sister began playing, "The Wedding March". Seth and his father, the best man, walked to the altar. Next were the bride, and her two sisters, Paula, the maid of honor and Nina, the bridesmaid, and Sarah's father, Lyle. As the ceremony began, Reverend Landis, the minister, began the vows. The minister responded with, "Who is to give this bride away?" Lyle spoke up with, "I do." Reverend Landis whispered to Lyle, "You may sit with your wife now." Lyle proceeded to the front pew and sat by his wife and Sarah's mother, Hannah. Hannah looked as beautiful as ever. She donned a blue lace trimmed hat, and blue suit with white blouse and small silver earrings.

The minister continued, "Sarah, do you take Seth to be your lawful wedded husband?" "Sarah, emotionally replied, "I do." The minister looking toward Seth and said, "Seth, do you promise to honor, cherish, and love this woman, Sarah, till death do you part?" Seth smiled, "I do." As the minister finished reading the vows, Sarah thought, "I will love Seth forever. He is the most wonderful person I have ever met." Mr. Landis replied, "Now, you may kiss the bride," Seth bent over and whispered, "I love you. You are so beautiful!" and kissed Sarah.

The minister motioned to the bride and groom, "You may turn around now. As Reverend Landis looked at the crowd, he spoke, "I want to introduce you to Mr. and Mrs. Seth Wiley. You are invited to their reception at Lyle and Hannah Linzee's house. See you all there! Starting with the first pew on the right, as you leave each of you can come by and congratulate the couple." After the couple walked down the aisle to the front door, Nina shouted, "Throw your rice!" Rice went everywhere.

After the wedding several of the friends from church headed over for the reception at Hannah and Lyle Linzee's, Sarah's

parents. Noah and Grace Wiley, Seth's parents, Seth's sister, Tiera, and his brothers, Blake and Gabriel, all joined at the Linzee's. Some of their relatives and their neighbors came to welcome the new couple, also.

Hannah's wedding cake turned out beautiful, with the trimming of the cake in blue roses over white and of course, there were mints and nuts from the local grocery, and some punch. Hannah had made the punch with a special recipe of lemon Kool Aid and grape juice. Grace remarked, "Hannah, how did you make your punch? Mmmm, this has great flavor." Hannah replied, "I always fall back to this recipe for my punch. I'll write the ingredients down for you, so you can have for your recipe file. In Sarah's hope chest, I placed this punch recipe. Sarah already copied several of our favorite recipes, and placed in the recipe box I made for her which she stores in her hope chest."

"While we are talking, I must let you in on a secret, Grace. I opened Sarah's suitcase, and I sewed the bottom of her gown by hand stitches. I bet she will get a kick out of that," Sarah continued. "That is so funny, Sarah, I wouldn't have thought of that," Grace replied.

Lyle nodded to Seth, "Look, Seth, to make sure your marriage works, remember to communicate. Communication is the key. Sometimes you need to talk to find out what's bothering your wife. A woman sometimes can get a little whiny, and she needs lots of lovin." About that time Noah walked over, "I heard that, Lyle and I agree a hundred percent. I just want to add; Never go to bed mad at each other. What ever problems should end at the break of day, and kiss at night and make up." Chuckling he added, "Making up is the best part."

After the wedding and the reception, Sarah and Seth headed back home and spent their first night at Seth's parents' home as

Mr. and Mrs. Seth Wiley. “Seth, I’ll put my gown on and I’ll be right out. Oh, My Gosh! Look what somebody did! The bottom of my gown is hand stitched together. That mom! It just had to be her. She opened my suitcase after I packed and sewed my gown bottom. Ha, this is so funny,” Sarah thought. Sarah and Seth started chuckling. “Your mom is pretty sneaky,” Seth stated, “stitching the bottom of the gown after you had packed.”

Snuggling and laying in bed, the feather mattress even made a more snuggly atmosphere. Seth spoke of their future. “Sarah, we are going to have a wonderful life together. We’ll have a big family, a beautiful home, and lots of love,” Seth assured. “How many children will we have?” Sarah questioned. “I want a big family. I have always dreamed of this, and now the beginning of a dream come true,” Seth replied.

II. Making a Home

When Seth and Sarah were first married, they lived with Seth's parents, Noah and Grace Wiley. "What in the world? Who's racing my sewing machine?" Grace asked inquisitively. Of course, Sarah was sewing and driving the machine just a little fast. "I'll slow down. Just didn't realize how fast I was going," Sarah answered. Many times Sarah wished she had her own home. Living with the in-laws was not that easy.

"Seth, I really appreciate your mom and dad giving us a home. I just wish we had our own. When do you think we can find something?" Sarah inquisitively asked. "Look, honey, I have been looking and I have a small house in mind a mile away. Needs some fixin, but I can do that. We'll check this place out very soon," Seth assured. Sarah was so excited. "Let's go look at the house tomorrow. We can walk from here. Will be a nice jaunt," Sarah recommended.

After looking at homes that were available in the neighborhood, this house turned out to be their first home, and within a year from living with the in-laws, they were able to move to this house. They were excited about their new home.

This definitely was not a new home, but a new home for them. Seth told Sarah, "Just decorate this home however you want it. The decorating can be your project. We will have a small garden, and you will be able to put food up. My mom has extra canning jars. We will just borrow some of them. She won't mind sharing them with us."

As he kept rambling on, he continued, "I'll set some posts. I think I'll just use a couple of railroad ties my dad has behind his barn shed. These ties were from an old railroad track a couple of miles away. When the railroad crew laid the new track, they just left the old ties in the ditch along side the new track. Dad and the neighbors loaded the ties on the wagon and shared the ties. I'll just attach some wire for a clothes line for your clothes. We will make this a home. Mom and dad will give us some starts of the peonies and iris's and any other flowers she has."

Sarah gave him a hug and a big kiss on the cheek and amiably replied, "I can't wait to get started. I know how I will decorate each room. I am choosing rose colors for my living room and greens for the dining room. I haven't decided on the bedrooms yet. I have plenty of time to figure this all out. I will make some new doilies for the living room, and some new dresser scarves for our bedroom. I have some beige broadcloth and some lace. I can embroider some flowers on them, maybe blue. I'll choose blue for our bedroom. I'm so excited!" Within the next few months Sarah decorated, painted and had each room sparkling clean. Her doilies had matched each room and brought out a homey atmosphere.

When time for their first born arrived, Sarah was in labor for twenty-two long hours. A midwife was scheduled to come to help with the birth. She lived a mile away, and was able to walk to the house and help with the delivery. The midwife's name

was Isabella, and she also helped the country doctor, Doctor Zorrick two days a week in town. Gathering up the hot water for sterilizing, cloths, and having everything ready, they waited. She sat and comforted and consoled Sarah, until the time arrived. “Easy Sarah, just push and it won’t be long,” she consoled. One last push the baby arrived, a little boy weighing in at 8lbs. 5 oz. and twenty one inches long.

Having the first grandchild was quite an honor. Having a baby boy would carry on the Wiley name. With a lot of discussion, Seth and Sarah agreed on the name Seth Lee Jr. “I hope the name Seth doesn’t mix the mail up when he gets older,” Sarah perceived. “Look Sarah if this does we will separate the mail with no problem. I think naming him Seth would be an honor to me,” Seth assured, “Anyway we will just call him by his middle name, Lee, and that will settle everything. Lee received lots of attention. Lots of pictures were taken. As Grace held Lee, Noah bragged, “Look at those cheeks! Those are Wiley cheeks. He is going to be a handsome young man. That’s for sure!”

Headed to church for the first time with Lee, their new baby, all were proud to introduce him to the congregation. “Oh, he is so sweet,” admired one of the neighbors, “Let me see his little toes.” She took his sock off and held his toes. “Look how little is feet are. Aren’t they so sweet,” she admonished. “I think he is going to look like his grandpa Wiley,” stated the pastor. “Oh, he is definitely going to have his grandpa’s smarts,” laughed Noah.

Grace and Noah sat in the last pew at the back of the church. As the congregation gathered to their pews, Sarah and Seth, carrying baby Lee, walked back and sat beside Grace and Noah. Baby Lee started crying, and Grace insisted Sarah feed him right there. Of course, Sarah as shy as she was had a hard time

breast feeding in church. She made it through the incidence, but would never forget that moment. She was glad they were sitting toward the back of the church.

With all the planning, the home was shaping up and Seth was working on the yard and the flowers. Seth cleared brush and did the needed repairs on the porch. Of course, Seth and Sarah wanted more children. When Lee turned two, Sarah became pregnant again. Seth was elated and very happy over the thoughts of another child. He was hoping for a girl, but after their first born, Lee, being such a joy, Sarah and Seth would welcome another boy. They both agreed as long as the baby was healthy. Winter time had arrived, and on February 8th the birth of their second baby had arrived. Seth headed to Dr. Zorrick's office after dropping Lee off with his parents. The birth and pregnancy had been an easy one, and Sarah was so thankful for that.

"I've been thinking about the name, Sarah. I really have a name I like. I think we should name him Gordon," Seth suggested. "I like that name too, Seth. I definitely know we should name him, Gordon. This name will fit him so well," Sarah quickly responded, "and I would like to use my maiden name, Linzee, for his middle name. "Gordon Linzee," that's what his name will be," Seth insisted.

Gordon was a colicky baby, but after getting through the first four months, Gordon was a very good baby. He never cried at night, and he slept all night right away. That was a blessing! He was so contented, and Lee was very helpful. Gordon began walking at one, and he followed Lee everywhere he went. Lee enjoyed his little brother's company, and he played with him and watched over him.

When Gordon was three, he still had bunches of curls in his hair, and some thought he was a little girl. "Sarah, we need to

cut Gordon's hair today," Seth demanded. "Okay Seth but I hate to cut his curls all off. All right, I guess. How about this afternoon?" she presented. In the afternoon Seth grabbed the clippers and they started cutting. Sarah silently went to the bedroom. She wiped a couple of tears from her eyes, knowing the haircut was of best interest for Gordon. The new look made him look much older and more like a boy.

Sarah made both boys cowboy outfits with chaps. Grandma and grandpa Wiley for Christmas the year before had given the boys toy guns and holster sets. After donning them in their new cowboy outfits, gun and holster sets, Sarah grabbed the camera. After placing the film, and getting the camera ready, she was ready to take some pictures. "Okay, let's take your pictures," Sarah beckoned. Gordon looking a little shy and Lee smiling as she snapped the picture of the two of them in their outfits.

Lee learned his lesson for honesty. On a crisp, breezy Sunday afternoon when visiting Hannah and Lyle Linzee, Sarah's parents, Sarah was complimenting her mother on the new knife sharpener, she had in her kitchen. After Lee heard the conversation, he decided his mother needed this sharpener, so he placed the hone inside the diaper bag. When Sarah got home, and reached for a diaper, there was the knife sharpener. She asked, "Lee, did you put this here?" "Yes, mom, but you liked it," he replied. "Lee, that is stealing. You will have to apologize to your grandparents, and give this back," she scolded.

The following day they all went over to the grandparents. "Okay, Lee what have you got to tell grandma and grandpa," Sarah asked. After all the blubbering, he finally got out that he was sorry, and he never stole anything again.

Lee loved climbing trees. He was very daring. He loved playing cowboys and Indians. "Lee, be careful," Sarah coaxed, "You had better not climb too high."

"I'm okay, momma. I'm a cowboy hiding from the Indians," he yelled back. At the same time, he slipped, fell and broke his leg. Seth was clearing brush and heard the commotion. "What's going on? "Seth asked as he came running. "Lee, fell from the tree, and I think he has broken his leg. He is in terrible pain," Sarah answered. Seth lifted Lee into the old Model A and Sarah grabbed Gordon. "We could drop Gordon off at your mom and dad's, Seth. I'll take him in the house and explain to her our plan," Sarah urged. "I don't see why not," Seth agreed. Headed to the parent's house, Sarah ran in the house and spoke with Seth's parents and explained what had happened. "Don't worry, Sarah, we will take good care of Gordon. I hope Lee will be all right," Grace affirmed. Getting back in the car, Lee cried, "I want my momma. My leg hurts!"

Seth and Sarah rushed Lee to Doctor Zorrick, the local and only doctor in downtown Covey. Covey was the nearest small town with a few stores, a doctor, a post office, and, of course, a hardware store. Lee was transferred to the hospital. "Seth and Sarah, we are going to operate and put a bar in Lee's leg. The bone is splintered and this is the only way we can make his leg strong enough to put pressure on the leg after the bone mends," Doctor Zorrick convinced them. "We have faith in you, Doctor Zorrick. You do what you think best," Seth replied. "After the surgery, Lee will be in the hospital a week before he can go home," Dr. Zorrick explained.

The stay in the hospital was a full two weeks, a little longer than they had anticipated. Sarah had arranged everything in his room for his comfort. She had prepared a stack of books on his nightstand, which his dad had made. She had some paper for sketching and artwork along with charcoal pencils and crayons.

Lee practiced sketching, and he became quite an artist. He sketched his grandma, Hannah, sitting in a a rocker. He did such a good job, Sarah said, "I just have to frame this. You have become a good sketch artist, Lee. Just continue to work at this. Sketching can become a great hobby for you."

Being laid up for eight months, he was soon as good as new. Gordon was young, but quite the helper. He helped Lee whenever he needed something. Lee read a lot, and loved to draw. Sarah had her hands full and plenty was on her plate.

Sarah, being a little nausea, realized she was pregnant again. Seth grabbed Sarah and placed his arms around her and murmured to her, "Sarah, another baby makes me very happy!" and Seth hugged and kissed her. "Me, too, darling," she replied.

In October the birth of a new baby had arrived. Sarah was washing the dishes when she realized she was going to give birth to her third child. She called for Seth, and they headed for the doctor's office. Preparation began for the birth. The nurse was running around getting all the blankets, cloths and other procedure equipment. She lay on the bed and after eight hours of labor, the Doctor Zorrick said, "It won't be long now, Sarah. Just a few minutes and your new baby will be here."

"Finally!" she said with a sigh.

The next baby was another beautiful little boy, Norman Campbell. Norman was named after his great uncle, Norman Wiley. His middle name was derived from his grandma Grace's maiden name. Using maiden names was a very common gesture for middle names. Norman was a very good natured baby. Seth and Sarah were so proud of their three boys.

Norman had a patch of freckles across his nose. As Norman grew a little older, he had a big curl on top of his head. Gordon spoke up and said, "Norman's hair looks like the guy that sets on the bench at Alec's gas and grocery, Mugsy Allen. Don't you think so, Mom?" "I think you are right. From then on all of them started calling him "Mugsy". Little did she know the name would stick with him throughout his school years.

"Sarah anything you need from Daisey's?" Seth inquired. "I'm walking down for a cup of coffee and chit chat with the farmers."

"Bring back some laundry soap and don't forget a sack of candy for me and the kids," she commented. About a half mile down the road was the corner coffee shop and combination small grocery store, Daisey's. The trees were green and flowing over the road. A gentle breeze was blowing as Seth strolled down the road. Memories of walking to school crossed Seth's mind. Seth began reminiscing of all the times he strolled this road from his home place to walk to school. He entered the store, and placed his hat and jacket on the coat tree.

Miss Daisey looked at Seth, "Seth, you look like you need a cup of coffee, cream and sugar, right?" "You bet, Miss Daisey. I'm needing a cup of coffee to get me going today. Just a tad bit of cream today. Last time I put too much cream, and my coffee taste more like milk. I have lots of brush to clear behind our home. "How's everybody doing?" Miss Daisey asked. "We are all fine, thanks. Oh, I need some laundry soap and small sack of candy, too. Sarah needs to wash diapers today. We are on our last dozen of diapers. She can hang them on the line today. With the nice breeze, the diapers will dry fast," Seth observed.

Seth drank his coffee and chit chat with all the farmers and loafers in the store. When he got ready to go, Miss Daisey handed him his supplies. He placed the bag full of groceries on the counter and reached into his pocket for his bill fold. "How much will that be, Miss Daisey?" Seth queried. "Just two dollars, Seth, just two dollars," Miss Daisey countered. He handed the two dollars to her and she slowly walked him to the door, "Now, you tell everybody in your household Miss Daisey said hello and here don't forget your sack, as she nudged him to grab the sack."

"Much abides, Miss Daisey, I'll make sure they get the message," Seth remarked. Some of the loafers yelled at Seth, "See you later, Seth." Seth waved his hand and replied, "You bet."

Sarah kept busy gardening and taking care of her family. Seth and Sarah were excited about a large family. Soon Sarah was expecting again. Of course, Seth, as always, was excited as he could be. With this pregnancy, Seth was hoping for a girl again. He just knew this was going to be a girl. All he could think of was, "I have three boys and maybe a little girl. What a wonderful world! I couldn't ask for anything more."

In the meantime, Seth had located a different home with a master bedroom and a bedroom for each of the children. A lot of farm ground, a big barn and shed, and lots of room for a garden and truck patch, a large garden grown especially for canning vegetables. Noah, his father, heard of this farmhouse through a friend. He thought this home would be perfect for their family. "Sarah, I must show you this home for your approval," Seth eagerly proclaimed.

After a quick journey to check the house out, Sarah loved the home also. "Seth, we will have so much more room in this house. Each of our children will have their own bedroom. There is so much room for the kids to play and the woods out back. This will be heaven to all of us. I am so excited," Sarah exhilarated. "Yes, honey, this is what we have been hoping for," Seth established.

After meeting with the owners and setting up the payments, they were ready to move. Both began gathering up and packing the dishes and glassware. Getting ready for the move, Seth looked at Sarah and said, "I hope this is not too much on you being pregnant and due in a couple of months."

"Don't worry, Seth, I will take it slow. We'll be fine. With all the help from the congregation of the church, I won't do any lifting," Sarah guaranteed him. Just as Sarah had said, the church ladies came and helped pack and move. Sarah provided a luncheon of ham sandwiches, potato salad, and fruit cocktail for them.

The move was completed. The boys were so excited with their new rooms. Sarah unpacked, and she began planning for the new quilts she would be making for their beds. The boys were allowed to choose the colors they wanted. "I want a red bandana quilt. Can you do that mom? I can call this quilt my Lone Ranger quilt. I can't wait," Norman declared. "What kind of quilt do you want Gordon and Lee?" Sarah curiously asked. "I don't know for sure yet Mom. I will think on it. I do like different shades of blue. Yeah, let's make mine blue, okay?" Lee confirmed. "I think I want brown and beige. Maybe I can keep mine clean with a darker color," Gordon insisted. "Just remember I can make different designs, like squares or stripes. Let me know if you have a different idea, and I will see what I can come up with," Sarah pried.

The boys were growing and able to fend for themselves. With another child on the way, Seth and Sarah couldn't wait to have a baby girl. Early January morning Seth was awakened by Sarah. "Get up and get ready," she said, "Take me to the hospital. I'm having pains." The birth of their new baby girl had arrived. Sarah was only in labor five hours. The birth of her baby girl was an easy labor. She was so tiny, and very delicate. "Look at those tiny little fingers and toes," the nurse noted.

"Isn't she so precious Seth?" Sarah bragged. "She is so little. I like the name Jeanie Flora. We'll use Flora for her middle name after my little sister, Flora. Flora had succumbed to typhoid fever when Sarah was a little girl. After having the boys, I will have to get use to holding a little girl, won't I?" Seth questioned. As Seth held her, he sang, "Jeanie with the light blue eyes, pretty light blue eyes, making up his own words as he went. Sarah started planning in her head, all the pretty little pink outfits she would stitch up.

The boys were so proud of Jeanie. "Let me hold her now, mom," Norm begged. "It's my turn," Gordon implored. "Look boys! While she is so little, let Lee pick her up and both of you sit down and we will let you hold her," Sarah stated. "Gordon you can hold her first," Sarah coached, "Now remember Norman and Gordon, be careful how you hold her. Keep your hands under her back and head. Remember all babies have a soft spot on top of their head. Don't ever forget that. Always support her back good. Babies are delicate, but they are stronger than what you think. Being so dependent on us, we have to all take good care of our little "Jeanie". Look! She's smiling at you!" Jeanie received a lot of attention over the next months. The boys still argued who could hold her first. They were very protective of her.

At the end of the day, Sarah propped her feet up on the foot stool in the living room and looked at Seth with great admiration, "Seth we are abundantly blessed, aren't we?" "Yes, we are truly blessed," Seth reiterated.

III. The Last Child

"Boys!" Hurry and get in the car! Grab a couple of blankets!" Seth shouted as he gathered up clothes for Sarah's suitcase. The old 36 Chevy never had a very good heater. "Those blankets may feel pretty good," said Seth. The end of November, 1945, and this evening was a chilly one at that. Sarah was not feeling the best this evening. Her baby was not due for another week. Being her fifth child maybe this baby would come a little early. Sarah was starting to have contractions, and this could be false labor. She remembered the contractions from the previous pregnancies, and how they would come and go. Today she just had this feeling that this was the day.

As the contractions progressed, Seth called the doctor. "Dr. Zorrick, Sarah's pains are ten minutes apart," Seth questioned. "Just bring her in and we will get ready for the birth," Dr. Zorrick told him. "Seth, we better hurry. My pains are getting closer," Sarah groaned as she began having another contraction. "Don't worry, honey, we will be there in about ten minutes. Just hang in there. It won't be long," Seth assented. "Seth, I can't wait much longer, hurry, please! Ohh! Another pain!" Sarah gasped.

Early morning Seth had taken two year old Jeanie to stay with her Aunt Nina, Sarah's sister. The three boys, Lee, age ten, Gordon, age eight, and Norman, age five, were supposed to be in the car ready to go. Instead they were arguing about who was going to sit by the windows. Finally Lee with his stern voice proposed, "Look, I'll sit in the middle and both of you can sit by the windows! Now quit fighting! Dad is going to be mad if you guys don't quit it. He has enough on his mind without this!"

The boys had gathered the blankets just as Seth instructed. Finally, they all calmed down, and started talking about the new baby. "I wonder if it's a boy or a girl?" Norman stated. "I hope it's a girl," Lee mentioned, "We need another girl for Jeanie to have a buddy and someone to play with."

A new clinic opened in downtown Covey. The Southside Clinic was the only clinic within miles of the small neighboring towns. Luckily, this clinic was only five miles away from their country home. Dr. Zorrick was the only doctor in the area and he moved his practice to the new clinic. He had delivered all of the other four children without complications. Seth and Sarah had a lot of faith and trust in him.

Pacing the floor outside the waiting room, Seth waited. The nurses kept reporting to him that everything was fine. The last time the nurse, Tia, stuck her head around the door and declared, "This won't be long now, Seth, just a few more minutes! I just think this one is going to be a girl. This baby has a fast heartbeat, and a girl has a faster heartbeat, so they say." Tia had been Dr. Zorrick's nurse for the last ten years. She had helped with the delivery of all of the other four children. Seth shouted back, "Yes, but those minutes are like a lifetime!" The boys were stunned by the anticipation of a new baby, and they were unusually tamed by the stay in the car. Eventually they succumbed to the safe haven of the warm blankets and fell asleep.

After two hours the baby was born. Seth could hear her cry for the first time from the waiting room. What a beautiful sound to him! She was beautiful with black hair and blue eyes. Most babies are born with blue eyes, and Seth hoped they would turn brown just like Sarah's. She had a pretty round face and pudgy cheeks. She looked just like the porcelain doll Aunt Nina had given Jeanie on her last birthday. Sarah had set it on a shelf in her room to preserve this doll as long as possible. Glass dolls would not last long with three brothers in the house!

Sarah's sister, Paula, had written a letter to them requesting she would like to pick the name for their new baby, if the baby was a girl, after her favorite movie star, Marlena Dietrich. Seth and Sarah decided upon Marly. "Don't you think we will like the name Marly, Seth? We will write Paula a letter and tell her we chose Marly which is very close to Marlena," Sarah accentuated. "Be sure and tell her we loved her idea," Seth added. "How about using Ann for her middle name? My great grandmother's first name was Anne. We will just drop the e," Sarah remarked. "Marly Ann, I like the sound of that," Seth phrased.

Seth walked into the room. There she was! She was the prettiest little baby looking up at him. Sarah was very proud as she said, "Here, Seth, do you want to hold her?" He held Marly close to him, as he whispered softly, "Hush, hush, go to sleep little baby." He was one happy man!

Seth was born December 12, 1912, and weighed twelve pounds and twelve ounces. He always joked that he was going to have twelve children, which never came to be. He realized amidst all that was happening, he better go check on the boys. He then went out to check on the boys and found they had fallen fast asleep.

Seth went back in to say good-bye and the nurses brought out the new baby again, and she was so darling. Seth fell in love with her immediately. "I'm going to leave now, Sarah. You and the baby take care. I love you both," Seth verified amorously as he whispered in Sarah's ear. "Okay," Sarah hugged Seth, "We'll be fine. You be careful. We'll see you tomorrow." He grabbed his coat from the coat rack, and he ventured home with the boys who were still asleep. He would just wait until they got home to tell them about their sister. He would pick Jeanie up the next morning and tell her about the new baby. He couldn't wait to get settled again as a family. With a quick thought he reminded himself, "I have a beautiful wife and five healthy children! Wow! What a wonderful life!"

Seth would wear his usual attire, bibbed overalls, and he would sit in his great grandmother's Viera Wiley's old oak rocker and sing to Marly for hours at a time. He handed Marly his pocket watch his dad had given him on his sixteenth birthday and let her hold it. She would look and gaze at the watch for a long time. Seth sang with great rythmn, "Three little maiden's walking on the ice, one slipped and fell, do, de, do," he sang. He sang and hummed hymns and different songs. If he forgot the words, he would just improvise by humming or the words do, de, do, and keep the rhythm. "Bringing in the sheaves, bringing in the sheaves, we shall all come rejoicing, bringing in the sheaves," his voice rang, "Shall we gather at the river, Shall we gather at the river, the beautiful, the beautiful river," he continued with the next song. He had a beautiful tone and sang many specials at church. After a few songs, Marly was fast asleep.

Sarah placed a bouncy seat between the kitchen and living room. Marly could watch her mommy wash, clean, and cook from both rooms. With five children, cooking and cleaning was a constant job. "Hi there, Marly, you little pumpkin, how's mommy's little sweetie?" Sarah shouted from the kitchen. Marly just started cooing and smiling, and she said, "Ma, ma," as she was wanting more attention and to be held. Marly was such a bright eyed spunky girl that everyone in the family gave her the nickname Spunky.

Sarah was either busy, cooking, quilting or baking, or cleaning. "Jeanie, do you want to help cut the cookies and put them on the sheet. I'll tell you what. I'll cut them. You pick them up and put them on the cookie sheet for me. Just go wash your hands. You can be my helper today. Marly can watch us," Sarah suggested as she mixed the dough. Marly sat in her chair jumping up and down jabbering away.

In the evening the atmosphere was cozy in the household. The family gathered around the old potbellied stove, with mom and dad smiling and so much in love. Gordon and Lee were reading, and Norman was building something with the tinker toys. Marly was rocking a doll, and Jeanie was reading a book.

Marly was very sensitive, and she cried easily. Whenever there was a long walk, she cried to be carried. "Carry me, carry me, daddy," Marly whined. "Grab hold my hands and jump, spunky," Seth spoke. Of course, daddy put her on his shoulders, and away they went. When she was a little older and could walk, she held his little pinky finger and followed him right along.

Since Marly was a little pudgier, she looked the same age as her older sister, Jeanie. Many had mistaken them for twins, Marly did have dark brown eyes, and Jeanie's were a beautiful baby blue like Seth's. Sarah dressed them identical, stitching up some cute little outfits. Sarah made the cutest little dresses of seersucker, cotton, or for the fancier dresses she used taffeta. She added a little rick rack or lace to touch them up. She went to the five and ten and picked up some ribbon for bows for their hair. She was quite a seamstress and saved a lot of money by sewing.

When Sarah wasn't able to get out to the store, Seth and the boys ran errands for Sarah; always taking her want list and buying all the little sewing notions and groceries she needed. "Don't forget white thread and white buttons at Ben Franklin, Seth," Sarah hollered as they headed to the car, "Remember we are out of sugar and flour; also you need some chicken wire. Norman, you and the boys help your dad not forget anything. When you get back, we'll have ham for supper. I'll fix some of our fresh sweet potatoes and we'll have our first picking of corn on the cob. I hope this year our corn has a sweet taste. Last year the corn was very bland. See you in a couple of hours. I might even make some bread pudding for dessert."

IV. Streamtown

Streamtown was an old mining town. In the earlier years the railroad track circled around the small towns. The steam engine came roaring up and picking up coal from the undermining coal shafts. Some of the local people worked in the mines, and they knew that the mines could be dangerous. When the men went into the mines, a small cage of canaries was taken down in the mines with them. If the canaries turned silent, there was a gas leak and the gas overtook the birds. The men scrambled out when the canaries passed out.

Jobs were scarce. Underground mining was a sure paycheck. Some wives were reluctant to have their husbands work in the mines, but for some this was not an option. Mining was the only job available. Luckily, Streamtown never had any explosions or accidents. Traces of old mining shafts were behind the Seth and Sarah Wiley's home. The old mining shafts were deep into the woods. These old mining towns and cinder piles were just memories now with just a small population residing in each small town.

The railroad was the best way to travel, and most small

towns had opera and gambling houses. A big booming town when located by the tracks. Streamtown had seventeen taverns during these times. There were barber shops, hardware stores, department stores, and fabric and notion shops.

These old towns were just faded memories now. The new population had no idea what a booming town this was at one time. Times had changed and these times were memories. If someone went through Streamtown now, you would never know this town had once been a busy bustling town.

When Seth and Sarah moved to Streamtown with three small boys, Truman was President and World War 11 was in full progress. Rationing of food and gas became a priority. "Seth, would you stop at the neighbors and see if they need anything at the store? We can get their groceries and ours all in one trip," Sarah advised. "Last week they ran some errands for me. I really appreciated the gesture," Sarah reminded herself. "Sure will, I might be a little longer, but I will hurry," Seth called out.

Everyone learned to manage with what was available and make ends meet. Every household learned to conserve and economize. In the country and those days, borrowing an egg or a cup of sugar was a very common gesture. Every neighbor was willing to help out, because each neighbor borrowed also.

Seth decided to purchase some bees and have their own honey. "Sarah, I have the boxes for the bees, and I will be bringing the bees to our place from our neighbor, Mr. Hines. He said I could have them, no charge. He said he wouldn't mind having a jar of honey. I hope this works for us. I love honey, don't you?" Seth commented, "You know honey is good for you. "I know honey is healthy, and I love honey on my toast," Sarah remarked, "My family never did have bees, so a new experience is waiting for me," Sarah voiced.

Seth spent a couple hours each day setting up the bees. Seth purchased wood, paint, and wire. Seth began building his boxes for the bees, ten in all. Seth had the boxes made, and he drove over to the neighbors. After conversing with Mr. Hines and catching up on the local news over a cup of coffee, he said his farewell and placed the bee boxes in the car and said, "Thanks, Mr. Hines, I sure hope this works out. I've never had bees before, but the sound of honey is sure good.

On a summer afternoon Lee and Gordon were playing near the bees. "Hey, Gordon, you want to dance on the bee boxes and make them buzz louder," Lee put forward. "Sure, sounds like fun," Gordon agreed. Gordon always agreed with Lee. He looked up to him and admired him. As Gordon was jumping up and down on the bees, a few got out of the box. Gordon had curly hair and some of the bees got in his hair. "Ow! I got stung on the head. Help! Help! The bees are stinging me," Gordon cried, "Mom, help! Dad, help!" Sarah heard the commotion and noise and ran outside. "Seth, come quick," she yelled. Seth came running. Sarah and Seth grabbed Gordon and pulled the bees out of his hair, washed his hair, and put a salve ointment on the stings. Gordon was not allowed outside the rest of the day, and he lay on the couch. Never would he get near the bees again. "For Pete's sake, Lee, didn't you and Gordon know the bees might get out, stomping on the boxes like that. You are lucky you only got stung once," Sarah reprimanded.

When the ole 36 Chevy wouldn't start, Seth walked into town with two gunnysacks to buy groceries. He carried them back, and in the winter pulled them over the icy roads. "Sarah, where is my wool scarf you crocheted me? I'll wrap the scarf around my neck and across my face. The scarf will protect my face from the cold winds. I'm going after some groceries. Make out your list," Seth exclaimed. "Wait a minute. Don't you think it's awful cold and windy?" Sarah echoed. Seth was tough and he knew they needed groceries. Standing in front of the wood stove, he stated, "I'll just dress warm, and I'll be back in no time. Would you make me some hot potato soup and have the soup ready when I get back?" "Don't forget Wheaties or Cheerios, dad," Norman reminded. Of course, he was wanting the prize in the box even though he did like the cereal. The whole family couldn't wait till he came back for all those goodies he was bringing. "Here's the list, Seth, and surprise us with some extra goodies," Sarah hinted.

As he headed back home all he could think of was the hot soup waiting for him. The sacks slid easily over the ice. Good thing he had on his insulated clothing and good treaded boots. The ice was very slippery, and the boots kept him from falling.

The boys rode "Ole Bess", the families' mare, into town to buy groceries when Seth couldn't make the trip to the store. Alec Jones, the manager of the main and only local grocery hardware store in Streamtown, bellowed from behind the counter, "Hi, boys!" as he put away his stock on the shelves, "I'll throw some licorice, cinnamon balls, and bubble gum in your sack today. I'm just putting it away now." He always managed to put extra candy in their five cent purchase bag of candy. All the groceries were put on "the bill" because Alec knew Seth was good for it.

In the spring on a grocery shopping spree at the grocery hardware store, Alec asked, "Hey, you boys going mushroom hunting today?" If you find some, I would like to buy a couple pounds. Just bring them by."

"All right!" Norman acknowledged hastily, "We will bring them in tomorrow! We're hoping to go this afternoon." Norman jumped at the chance to make some fun and easy money. He was so excited. This would be a little spending money for them. Norman wanted a new Red Ryder b-b gun that he had seen at the hardware store in Covey.

Norman couldn't wait to get home to tell his mother that Alec wanted some mushrooms. As they entered the door, Sarah was pressing some clothes. First she heated the old iron on the cook stove, and then pressed the pants. She was on her last pair. "Mom, guess what?" Norman outburst, "Alec wants some mushrooms and he will pay us for them." Sarah motioned toward the breadbox. "Grab two or three of those sacks in the breadbox. They have holes in them. The old saying is if you pick mushrooms, the holes in the sacks allow the spores to drop to the ground to produce more mushrooms next year."

"Hopefully we can find enough for ourselves and Alec," Norm excitedly exclaimed. Lee added, "I can't wait to eat them." Sarah spoke out, "Don't forget to look under the mayflowers. We've had some rain, and I think you will find plenty." Finding mushrooms under the mayflowers was easy for Sarah. The mayflower was about a foot high with leaves shaped like a umbrella. The mayflowers had grown just the right height, which meant the mushrooms were up.

Lee, Norman, and Gordon all headed to the woods with their sacks. "Grab a stick for a cane. Dad always does, and he just walks in the woods and takes the cane. He'll point and say pick that one. Hey, let's look around that old dead elm," Lee said, "At least it looks like the old elm is dying, and that should be some good mushroom hunting."

"Found one!" said Lee, "Great Scot, I found another one!" he retorted. "I'm coming," said Norman. "Oh, My gosh! Look at this one!" shouted Gordon. "I think I found the biggest one," yelled Norman, "and I hope we have enough sacks for all of these. Look, these are under the mayflowers just like mom said. I think we will have enough for us and Alec both. I can't wait to show everybody. We'll come back and hit this same spot tomorrow." The boys were excited over all the mushrooms. Heading back home, Lee avowed, "Maybe mom has camera film and we'll take our pictures besides the mushrooms."

"Sounds good to me," Gordon agreed.

The next day Norm and Gordon had a chance to go back to the same mushroom spot. "Don't forget extra sacks," Sarah recommended from the kitchen before they left. Out they headed to their favorite spot, which they would never tell the location. After they arrived, Norman shrieked, "Holy cow, there is a clump of five, and look over there at that huge one!" They must have popped up overnight," Gordon wailed. "Good thing we have plenty of sacks. I'm glad mom told us to take the extra sacks. I hope dad fries them up tonight or tomorrow. I love the way he fries them. Holy Smokes! Makes me hungry now," recalled Gordon.

Lots of hard work was ahead for the summer and fall. Trees were cut with a crosscut saw operated by two people, one at each end. Seth was at one end and Lee at the other. Norman and Gordon cleared the brush and stacked the wood. "Grab a hold, Lee," Seth hollered as they both began tugging and pulling. "We need to cut these three trees down before dark, and split, load, and haul them to the house. Two people would push and pull until the trees were cut. The logs were trimmed and cut for firewood. The wood was split with an ax, and cut the right size for the old wood stove. Bess was harnessed up with the sled behind, and the logs were loaded on the sled.

While Lee and Seth cut the wood, the boys, Gordon and Norman, hauled the wood to the house. "We'll stack the wood and surprise dad when he gets to the house," Gordon ordered. "Yeah, he'll be surprised we stacked the wood so nice," Norman added, "Man! I'm getting tired and hungry. I hope mom has some of the good fried steak she makes. I can just taste her mashed potatoes and gravy. She said she was going to make a gooseberry pie, one of my favorites!"

The wick on the kerosene lamp was getting shorter, and the kerosene lamp was almost empty. The best lamp was the high velocity lamp given to them by Noah, Seth's father. This lamp was a Christmas present the year before. Reading in the evening, Seth and the family gathered around the high velocity lamp.

"Dad," inquired Norman, "Gosh, dad I forgot to shut the barn gate. Did you shut the barn gate when you left?" He didn't want the cows to get out. "Don't worry, son, I checked them all," Seth drawled, as he was chewing his tobacco. To relax Seth placed his five-gallon bucket next to him, and chewed and spit. "Seth, take your bucket and set in the wash room tonight. Don't leave it in the house," Sarah reminded Seth. Sarah never allowed the bucket to stay in the house.

"Lee, which one of you put the bucket of water over the door in the barn," Seth exclaimed. "Well, did you get wet dad?" Norm asked and let out a loud roar. "We were only trying to surprise you, dad," Gordon reiterated. "Did I get wet? That water scared the livin daylights out of me! That's okay but next time I'll get you," Seth validated.

After a busy day, the family all retired at eight in the evening, as five o'clock rolled around pretty fast. "Boys, I have the alarm set for five. We have to get the milking done and in the milk cans before seven. The milk man will be here anytime after seven," Seth proclaimed. Milk and egg sales provided a little income for the family. The income was enough for the grocery bill. "Tomorrow, Mr. Cobbs, the bread man, delivers bread, and we can pay the bill with our cream and milk check," Sarah noted, "I want to get eleven loaves of bread, as last time we ran out, and he never delivered to us one week because of bad weather. We'll try some of the new wheat bread. Doesn't that sound good? We will get some glazed yeast doughnuts, too. We might try some of the iced cake donuts, too."

V. Country Life

"Girls, we're going outside under the big oak tree in the back yard. The boys are playing ball and we'll watch them. I'll bring a blanket to sit on. I also made some cherry Kool Aid and a snack for us," Sarah proposed. "What kind of snack, mom, did you bring?" Jeanie asked. "I made some cinnamon bars. You can sample this new recipe, and let me know if you like the recipe," Sarah asserted.

Marly with her doll, Jeanie with her book, and Sarah went out under the old oak tree. Little Jeanie tried to keep up with her brothers, but soon took refuge under the big oak tree with her mother and sister. Sitting on a patch of clover, Sarah stated, "Look, Jeanie, have you ever found a four leaf clover. Let's look for one. The old saying is a four leaf clover will bring you good luck."

"Mom, look, look, I found one," Jeanie shouted. "When we go inside we'll place the clover between the pages of a book to preserve the clover," Sarah said. Sitting in the back yard on the blanket, the beautiful view of the farm overlapped Sarah's thoughts. Sarah sighed and said a prayer, "Thank you God for these many blessings."

"Tonight Marly, we will catch lightning bugs," Jeanie explained. "I love to catch lightning bugs, sis," she replied. Sarah gave them a jar and they collected about twenty. Jeanie decided to let them go. "Mom I want to let them out. I am afraid they will die," Jeanie confirmed. "Come inside and we will get a couple of spools and rubber bands and make them walk. You just get a stick, a spool, and rubber band and wind the stick with the rubber band," Sarah presented. "We will get some large buttons and wind them up with a rubber band and watch them go," she added.

"Mommy," blubbered Marly, "Can I sleep with you tonight?" "You can tonight, but remember a little castor oil on a heel tomorrow," asserted Sarah. Discipline that Marly hated was castor oil on a heel of bread. Castor oil is a oil that helps to keep you regular. A little never hurt anybody, but has a very nasty, oily taste. Marly would not sleep in her bed, so she was allowed to sleep in her mom and dad's, but she had to eat a heel of bread with castor oil on it the next day. She was five years old now, and she learned to sleep in her bed real fast after that. Sarah had such a busy, hard-working life that there had to be rules. Sleeping in your own bed was one of them.

Sarah was very crafty. She made all the boys cowboy shirts, pants, and chaps. She even made them hats. Taking a wire and putting around the rim made the hat brim stand out. The neighbor children loved coming to play at their house and were envious of the homemade western outfits, even though some of the mother's had ordered western cowboy outfits from the Spiegel's catalog for them.

"Seth, I am going to get some film for my camera next time we go into Covey five and ten. I need to take some pictures. I have a new photo book your mother gave me for my birthday.

I must get started filling the book soon," Sarah spoke as Seth listened on. "Sarah, we will just go into Covey today. We don't want our children to grow up without any pictures," Seth responded.

On May 1 of every year, Sarah allowed the children to go barefoot, but not until then. Sarah drilled, "You have to wait until May first, or you will get sick." Marly loved walking on the grass with her bare feet, and grass blades were so soft. She also loved wading through the mud puddles after the rain. From being outside and playing so much, Jeanie and Marly had deep tans.

Norman, Gordon, and Lee headed down to the barn, sleepy, and trying to wake up. "Hey, Norman, if you milk Bessie today, I will the rest of the week," pleaded Gordon. Norman shouted back, "Gee willikers, I don't want to, but all right, but remember you milk her the rest of the week." Bessie was the meanest of the cows. She gave them a hard time trying to kick when they were milking. The boys alternated turns milking her.

Seth had made some homemade stools. A flat piece of wood was nailed to the top of a log. Norman placed his head into Bessie's belly, and if she started to kick, he would have a head start to pull the bucket away. "Aw, shucks! She kicked my milk bucket over. Now I will have to start over. If she keeps this up, let's put the hobbles on her. Okay, Gordon?" Norman begged. Gordon shrieked, "Gosh darn, I spilt my milk, too. Let's put the hobbles on now. We can't afford to lose any more milk." With the legs confined, Bessie could not kick and you would not lose any milk.

Jeanie and Marly followed Norman and Gordon to the barn while they did the milking. "Jeanie let's play beauty shop," Marly offered. "Okay, I have two barrettes in my hair we can use," Jeanie commented. Marly and Jeanie braided the cow's tails with their own barrettes. Usually the cows switched their tails to swat flies off of their backs, and the barrettes went flying somewhere in the barn. "Oh, piffle, I lost another barrette," cried Jeanie, "Help me find it Marly, hurry, mom will get mad if I lose these new barrettes."

"I found it! I found it!" Marly screamed. They continued playing beauty shop, and would commence to style the hair.

Norman gestured for Jeanie to come closer and closer. Norman squirted the girls and the cats with the milk. He said, "Gotcha," and he laughed and laughed. "I'm going to tell mom you're wasting the milk, and you will get in trouble," cried Jeanie.

The boys brought the milk to the house. Sarah poured the milk into the separator. "I want you boys to help me with the milk this morning. I need to separate the cream from the milk, and we will take turns churning the cream into butter," Sarah ordered. One spout would pour out the cream used to churn butter, and she also made cottage cheese. The extra milk was poured into milk cans to sell. The milk man came two to three times a week. Selling milk gave extra income for the family and provided a little extra spending money for Sarah.

"Don't forget to gather the eggs tonight, Mugsy," Sarah reminded, "I need eggs for the angel food cake I am going to make. Also, I want to make some deviled eggs."

"Okay mom as soon as I finish reading my Lone Ranger comic book. I'm on the last page," he answered back. With a few chickens, there was no hen house. The hens roamed all over the yard and barn. Finding the nest to gather the eggs sometimes was hard, but eventually you knew where to look for the nests.

VI. Moving the Brooder House

Just about time for the school bus to drop the kids off, Sarah could hear Marly shouting, "Mom! Mom! What time is it? Is it time for Lee to get home?" "You have ten minutes. Just be patient Marly. I will tell you when you can go. Remember, have patience. Count to ten," Sarah urged. Sarah sang, "Have patience, have patience." A big old maple tree marked the entrance to the lane of their home. Lee and Marly were best buddies, and she couldn't wait until Lee came home from school. When the time arrived, she sat on a small stump next to the tree and waited for the arrival of the bus.

"Boys, we are going to cut your hair tonight," Seth ordered. "Oh! No! I hate having my hair cut. The clippers hurt," Norman whined. The clippers did manage to pull a few hairs. Seth was a little rough cutting hair. He had three boys' hair to cut and all the chores to do before dark. "We'll start with Lee and go down according to your age. Gordon you be ready," Seth gestured. After cutting Lee and Gordon's hair, now was time for Norman. "Your turn, Norm, we'll soon be done. Come and get in the chair," Seth stated as he gestured for Norman to sit on the chair.

Norman, with a frown on his face, unwillingly went over to the chair and sat down. "Ouch, that hurts!" Norman whined. Finally the task was done. "Sarah, don't you like the way I cut the boys' hair so short? This hair cut should last all summer," Seth asked as he looked at Sarah. "That's great, Seth. I know the boys will be glad too," Sarah answered.

"I know we have to get the brooder house ready, Sarah, but I think I will move it closer to the house," Seth suggested. A brooder house is a small little house to raise new little chicks. The brooder house was in need of some repair. With Sarah's permission, Seth decided to move the brooder house closer to the house. "Sarah, you will be closer to the little chicks if I move the brooder house. Maybe the boys can help keep the chicks watered and fed," Seth instructed.

On a Saturday afternoon, Seth was moving the brooder house. The baby chicks were ordered from the downtown Covey hardware. "How many chicks are they going to deliver, Sarah?" asked Seth. "I think this year we are receiving ninety-five. They will deliver on Friday. We need to get the brooder house ready," Sarah requested. Sarah loved raising little chickens to butcher. She placed heat lamps over the tops of them to keep them healthy and warm. These little chicks were so cute. They were so soft and furry. In a few months they were slaughtered for the meat. Renting a locker in Covey, Sarah was able to fill the locker full with chicken, beef, and pork. Country fried chicken is about the best eating ever, especially Sarah's.

The children were in the front yard. As Seth was moving the brooder house the tractor slipped out of gear, and began rolling back down the hill toward their dad. He was working away on the door and never even noticed the tractor rolling toward him. The children screamed, "Look out, dad! The tractor is rolling and going to back up on you!" He looked up just in time to duck.

He was saved by the small gap below the tire of the tractor. The brooder house was crushed on one side. Whew! How close!! Seth decided to quit for the day. Seth was safe and not injured. He was a little shook up, but only had a small scratch on his arm. The evening was a peaceful quiet evening for just plain relaxing and taking a deep sigh of relief that all went well.

Norman and Gordon were mean to the chickens. "Norman, I will race you to see who can run their bicycle over the first chicken to squat," Gordon cried out. "Undoubtedly I bet I win," Norman replied with anxiety. When the chickens squatted, the boys ran over them with their bicycles. The boys were in deep trouble when they hog ringed the chicken combs; and when they went into the hay mow with the chickens and dropped them into the basketball goal.

"Okay, boys, I want you to clean and scrub the old hog house down by the barn, and then the one out by the chicken coop. Next time you will remember how to treat the chickens. I want you to think about what you have done while you are scrubbing," Seth ordered. When Seth saw the boys playing basketball with the chickens, each got a switching with a stick. Seth just let the wrongdoer pick out his own switch. Seth said, "Just pick your switch, and remember this hurts me more than it does you."

Gordon insisted Jeanie go outside with him on a cold wintry day. "Come on Jeanie," Gordon coaxed his little sister. "Get your boots on, and we're going to have fun," he prompted as he put on her sweater. She did as she was told and sat in the wagon as he pulled it. With the fresh snow on, Gordon pulled Jeanie for a ride in the wagon. "Are we going to make a snowman?" she responded. He pretended they were in the wild West in a covered wagon. The water was rivers, and her weight in the wagon helped to make the tracks for the road. They were on the lookout for Indians, and both of them had so much fun. Jeanie got so cold, but she kept on going. "Look, Jeanie! Look at that squirrel! He's hiding a nut. Did you ever wonder how a squirrel in three months could find the nuts he hides? Don't ask me how, but they remember. Aren't squirrels fun to watch?" Gordon questioned. "Yeah, I wish I could hold one, but it would bite me," Jeanie replied.

On November 28, 1952, Marly turned seven. Sarah sent Norman with Seth into town. Seth had to pick up some hardware items. Sarah secretly motioned for Norman to come to her. She said, "I want you to go with your dad. While he is in the hardware store, you run over to the five and ten Ben Franklin store. I want you to pick out a present for your sister for her birthday. Norman did as his mother requested, and purchased a birthday present for Marly. The most beautiful necklace and bracelet set, pink and alternating with pearls were awaiting her. In the evening Sarah beckoned for Marly. "Okay, Marly, close your eyes," Sarah remarked. "Okay, Mommy, I'm not peeking," as she gradually opened her eyes, jumping up and down she shouted, "I love it! These beads are beautiful."

VII. Christmas

On the evening of November 1, 1952, the day was cold and wintry. You could hear the wind howling and blowing against the window. The potbelly stove was going full blast. The stove pipe was burning red hot. There was a warm feeling inside. You could smell the freshly baked sugar cookies, and hear the meat sizzling in the kitchen.

Sarah hollered from the kitchen, "Marly, don't get too close to the stove pipe, or you'll singe your hair again!" She had done this in the past, and her mother knew she had better warn her again. Sarah was just about ready to call them for supper. She placed her scalloped potatoes on the table and retrieved the meat from the oven where she had placed the meat to keep it warm. "Come and get it, Seth, supper is ready. Get the kids and come on before the food gets cold!" her voice rang as she wiped her hands on her apron. She always wore an apron. She had sewn many for herself, but this one was hand sewn by her mother. The chicken feed that was ordered for the little chicks came in colorful cotton sacks. Sarah washed them up, and made aprons, tablecloths, and many other household articles. She even made herself some house dresses.

Christmas was coming soon. Ordering presents from the Alden's or Spiegel's catalog was the best way to shop for rural folks. Seeing big boxes hanging on the mailbox, you would know the presents had arrived. Being young, there was still a little question about Santa Claus for Marly, especially when Gordon told her to look out the window, and she could see Santa on his sleigh with Rudolph pulling and leading the reindeer. He said, "I can see him, can't you?"

Seth and the boys went to the woods and chose their Christmas tree, a cedar tree. Lee called out, "Look, dad, how about this one?" This tree was perfect shaped, but just a little thin, but with the decorations it would be perfect. "Okay, son, I'm bringing my saw, and we will cut it down. You hold the tree," as he raced over to their area and began cutting. The boys carried the tree to the house, and put the stump into a pot of rocks for stability.

The children and Sarah strung popcorn, and colored and cut paper strips for garland. After pasting the garland strips together, they stranded them over the doorways and some on the tree. Cranberries were stranded with a needle and thread, and this made a colorful decoration. All the decorations they made were added to the tree, plus a few they had purchased from the five and dime the years before. Sarah pointing at the left side of the Christmas tree, said, "We need another strand of garland over here on this side."

"The top does look a little bare on that side," Lee agreed. A wonderful Christmas, indeed, it was.

The boys received games and new sleds. Carom was one of the games, a large board with shooters and rings. The board games they received were Parcheezi and Scrabble. Jeanie received some new craft items, colored pencils and drawing paper and Marly loved her present that year, a new doll with brown hair, dressed in pink with little pink rollers for her hair, a pink and white dress and bonnet to match. The vinyl smelled so fresh and new; also new furry, fluffy hats and gloves to match their hand me down winter coats from their cousins.

Getting their coats and new hats they received for Christmas on, the girls entered the bus. A lot of teasing occurred on the bus. As the girls entered the bus, the bully of the bus, Rodney, shouted, “Look at their new hats!” “Be quiet Rodney and sit down. Leave my sisters alone. A big guy like you! No kiddin! Stop it!” Gordon ordered. Rodney sat down and never said a word.

The week end was snowing like crazy. This year the winter was hard, and lots of snow which was a perfect setting for the boys. The boys got their new Christmas sleds, and they were off. They went down the steepest hill back behind the barn. They were able to make an ice snow fort, which took them forever to build. As Gordon came around the corner of the big ash tree someone yelled from the other tree. “Look out!” the voice echoed. He was hit in the face with a big snowball. Norman started running with Gordon not far behind with a big handful of snow. “Look, Mugsy, I’ll get you. You can’t outrun me,” Gordon shrieked. “Oh Shoot! Norman outburst, “I got to get out of here!

VIII. More Country Fun

The boys dug a cave at the top of the side of a hill behind the barn. The first cave was not very big, and after the first rain, this cave washed away. The next cave was bigger, and mud steps led to the top of the hill where the cave was located. "Did you bring the five gallon bucket for us to build a fire?" asked Lee. "I'll get the bucket and some food and I'll be right back," replied Norm. The cave could hold all of them and the fire felt pretty good on a cold day. You could join this club for a marble.

"Look, Marly, you can join the club for a marble," stated Norman. "But I have a marble, and so I can join. I have a cat-eye marble," Marly assured. "Great Ceasar's ghost! Where did you get that cateye marble, Marly?" Norman swiftly asked. "I found it," Marly answered. "Geminy Christmas! Look at this marble. Sure you can join," Norman confirmed. So she got into the cave which was only big enough for four or five people. At least she got to join.

The boys began making another cave, and made this one bigger. "Let's get some grape vines and smoke them. Gordon, you cut them and get them ready, and I'll look for some horse weed to smoke," said Lee. Gordon did as he was instructed fetching the grape vines and cutting them the right length. Lee, Barry, Gordon, and Chuck all gathered in the cave and smoked their grapevines. Norman entered the cave and said, "What are you doing? I want one, hey, give me one." So Norman started smoking a grapevine also. "My throat is getting sore," Norman stated, "I think I'll go to the house. See ya, guys." Away he went. The others ended up with a sore throat also.

The boys hauled walnuts and let them dry on top of the metal roof of the wood shed. Gordon made a tunnel down hill and smacked the walnut and let the walnut run down the hill. By the time the walnut reached the bottom of the tunnel, the shell had fallen off. Bess, the old mare, pulled the sled with walnuts on it. Putting the walnuts on the lane for cars and tractors to peel them with the tires was another way to haul them. They were able to hull them faster.

After the nuts dried out, they were picked out of the shell, and used for baking or adding to candy. "Jeanie, I can't wait to have some chocolate fudge with these nuts," Marly voiced as Jeanie kept plucking away. "I can't wait to have some divinity," Jeanie replied. Sarah made the best chocolate and peanut butter fudge. She also made great divinity and popcorn balls. "You can leave the nuts in the shell and we will pick the nuts out later," Sarah called, "Just crack as many as you can. I plan on making divinity and popcorn balls for the bazaar next week.

The electric company was installing electricity into more rural homes. Being one of the last, finally the time had arrived. New electrical wires were installed heading right above the entrance of the kitchen door. The new electricity was an exciting time for all of them. "Just think, we will have lights by the week end. No more kerosene lamps. This will be heaven," Sarah shouted as she looked at Seth. "We will get us a radio,"

Seth acclaimed. "Mom, can I get a radio. I want to listen to Hopalong Cassidy and Roy Rogers and some of my other Westerns," Norm asked. "We'll probably get a radio, but Noah said he may have one to give us. Grace gave him one for his birthday, and he doesn't need two. We'll check with Noah next time we visit," Sarah convinced.

Sarah never drove much, but once in a while she would get brave enough to drive to their mail box which was a half mile west of their home. After getting all the children in the car, they were off. "You all sit still. We're going to the mailbox to get our mail," Sarah ordered. All was fine until coming back she veered off the road. "Oh, nuts! Look what I have done. We are in the ditch!" Sarah screamed. "Let's walk home, mom, and we can come after the car when dad gets home from work," Gordon persuaded her. They all walked home and Sarah never drove again.

When Seth came home, Sarah explained what happened. Seth and Lee went after the car. After a little pushing and tugging, the car was out of the ditch, and both headed home. Seth consoled, "Don't worry, Sarah, this could happen to anybody. Just remember to be more careful next time."

Even with Seth's assurance, Sarah was not confident with driving. Sarah did not want to drive again.

IX. Some Work and Some Play

"Dad, I have a flat tire on my front tire. Can you help me patch the inner tube sometime today?" Norman asked. "Son, as soon as I get home from the store, we will fix your tire. I'll show you how, so you can learn. Next time you will be able to fix your own inner tube," Seth offered. Seth repaired the tire and at the same time, instructed Norman how to fix it.

"Mom, do you care if Lee, Gordon and I subscribe to Vippert's Seed Company catalog? We want to sell seeds for some extra money and free gifts," Gordon asked. "Go ahead. Just remember the seeds are your responsibility," Sarah answered, "Keep track of who you sell to, and when the seeds come in, you will have to separate and deliver them yourselves." With their mother's permission, Norm and Gordon subscribed to the seed catalog, Vippert's Seed Company. They rode their bikes in and all around the neighborhood selling seeds after school. Many times they would stare at night at the gift they would receive for selling so many seeds. Depending on how many seeds were sold would depend on what gift bracket you could pick from. Some items were pretty nice gifts, as a b-b gun or a knife. With a few extra seeds, Gordon was the one who planted them. He was in the highlight of his glory, as he always loved experimenting with flowers and gardens.

Gordon purchased his mom flowers, baby tears, philodendron and ivy at the local five and ten. "Mom, I'm home?" Gordon exclaimed as he carried the pot of flowers. "I got you something," he said. "What in the world have you got?" Sarah exclaimed. He held the flower pot out, and Sarah gave him a big hug and put the flower on the kitchen sill. "Thank you so much, Gordon, those baby tears are my favorite flower. I will transplant all three into separate pots.

Land sakes, Gordon, you didn't have to spend your money on me," she stated as she wiped a tear from her eye. "I wish I had more money, so I could buy more things like the neighbors," Gordon confirmed. "Look, Gordon, we are so blessed, and the grass isn't always greener on the other side," Sarah reminded him.

Sitting around the dinner table Seth opened a suggestion, "Boys, did you know that I can make a kite that stays up for days? It is called a box kite. We'll make one tomorrow. Did you save the string from the feed sacks, Sarah, like I asked?" "I put the big ball of string in the top of the cupboard shelf in the wash room. It's right by the laundry soap. You'll see it," Sarah input. "Gosh, dad, I can't wait," Mugsy responded "Dad, you can make a kite that stays up for days? Great Scott, I wonder how many days?" Lee asked. "Well, I bet two or three," Gordon interrupted. "Tomorrow we need to get some horse weeds for the frame. You boys can help me get the horse weeds. I'll find the string in the wash room and we'll start making our kite tomorrow," Seth acclaimed.

Seth and boys tackled their job. "First we have to get the

horse weeds," Seth ordered again, "After that we will get some strong brown paper. I have some in the wash room we can use. After getting the horse weeds, Seth showed them how to make four squares with twine, make the shape of a box and attach a string with a paper tail. The wind is perfect today. We won't have any trouble flying our kite today." After getting the job all done, Seth ran with the kite and showed them how to get the kite in the air, and the kite went up. "Wow, look how high the kite went!" Jeanie breathlessly spoke. Her eyes were so very wide and in awe. The third day the kite was still up. "Good Night! Dad, the kite is still up," Gordon mentioned at breakfast. After the third day, the kite was gone. This was a kite experience the family would never forget.

After all this wind, I know we are going to get some rain. The farmers will be glad to get a little rain, since it has been so dry. After a full day of rain, Norman ran inside and said, "Mom, dad, come quick. You have to see this beautiful rainbow!" With all of them running outside, they admired the brightly colored rainbow. Jeanie spoke, "Look! The end of the rainbow follows in our field." Sarah replied, "Didn't you know the old saying is a pot of gold at the end of the rainbow."

The seasons were very predominant in Indiana. Each season was so special. The spring was very green and new leaves, and smell of fresh blooms from the trees and shrubs. Summer was windy, nice breezes, and a sunny time. Fall was so colorful with the different trees turning all shades of browns, oranges, and greens. Winters were beautiful with the fresh white fallen snow. The big snow flakes dropping on the ground, but yet the winter weather was blistery, windy, and sometimes very cold, even a few blizzards.

In the winter time, Lee rode his bicycle from house to house selling his rabbits. He was able to hunt and earn a little extra money at the same time.

One neighbor, Mrs. Hines, did not really want to buy a rabbit at that time. Lee was so cold and hungry, she did anyway. Instead of paying the usual dime he charged, she offered a nickel which he accepted. She served him milk and cookies, and she let him warm up next to the wood stove. "You hurry and get home, Lee. You better get home before dark. We are supposed to get four inches of snow. Would you mind helping to shovel some snow for me later this week?" she stated as she kneaded the bread on the breadboard, "I'll send you home some cinnamon rolls when you come back and help clear the snow." As he rode his bike, the snow flakes began to flow. Big snowflakes hitting his face, but he would soon be home to the warm potbellied stove. Ahhh! That sounded so good!

As he rode with the rabbits in the basket by the handlebars, he alternated his hands from pocket to pocket to keep them warm. It was a very cold ride, but all he could think about was what his mom was cooking for supper. Between selling rabbits and garden seeds, Lee hoped to buy a new Red Ryder air rifle.

Nothing was better than a good ole corncob fight. Some good fights around and about the barn existed. To make the corncobs fly better, a feather was inserted in the end of the corncob. With all the chickens around, there were plenty of chicken feathers gathered on the ground. "Our side is the west side of the barn," Gordon insisted, "You get the east side and the battle begins. Get in your places!" Gordon hollered. "Lee and Barry are on my side," Norm announced, "You get Chuck and Spike."

"Look out!

Norm," Barry cried, "One coming from the side of the barn. That was close. "Ow!! I got hit in the head," yelled Gordon. After a few rounds, Spike yelled, "Holy Mackerel! Tie, Tie! It's a tie! Let's quit this time and we can have another round again tomorrow. I need a rest."

"Lee, you know where the grapevines are in the woods by the old elm tree where we fish?" Gordon inquired. "Yes, why Gordon?" Lee asked.

"I want to cut the grapevines. There are two of them. We will swing on them. There is a hill and you can get a running start," Gordon answered, "I'll bring my knife and we'll start cutting. Come on Norm, you can come with me," Gordon declared. The long walk in the afternoon was very hot. After an hour of cutting, finally the grapevines were ready. Getting a running start, and then plopping in the water hole; Sure felt good to be in that old water hole. "You go first, Gordon," Norm called out. "Okay, here goes," Gordon yelped. "Wow! Get a running start."

"That looks like fun. Let me try," Norm input. All afternoon they swung on the vines, coming home exhausted. The trip home only made them very hot again. Sure was good to be home.

"Son, my dad has a "long tom goose" gun he wants to show you," Seth pronounced. "Can I shoot the gun, dad, can I?" Lee asked. "We'll see, son. I'm going over there today. You want to ride with me?" Seth expressed. "Sure, dad. I'm excited to see this gun. Is this the gun his great-grandfather gave him?" Lee uttered. "I think so. We'll leave after dinner," Seth phrased.

As Lee and Seth drove up to the house, Noah was on the porch cleaning the gun. "Can I shoot it grandpa, can I, uh?" Lee begged. "Calm down, son, of course, he'll let you shoot it," Seth consoled. After putting some cans on a fence post, Noah handed the gun to his grandson. "See if you can hit those cans," he said. Lee shot the gun and fell backwards. "Man, I wasn't expecting that," Lee screamed. "This gun has a kick back," Noah answered, "Are you okay? I forgot to tell you that the gun had a kickback."

Slingshots were made from the tongues of old shoes and inner tubes. "All right, boys, I see a willow tree. We'll make the fork from a willow branch, I have my pocket knife and we will make each of you a slingshot," Seth coached, "I have some inner tube strips and a couple of shoe tongues. "We'll make a couple extras for your friends. Take your slingshot when you go frog hunting," Seth stated.

Seth was always good to the neighbor buddies making them slingshots, too and repairing bicycle tires. Seth started making slingshots and ended up with ten in all. A trip to the creek with your slingshot made for some good frog hunting. Sarah could fry up the frog legs so you would only ask for more. "I have plenty of worms and safety pins and a few fishing hooks," Gordon mentioned to Norm as they carried their tackle boxes. "I feel like this is going to be a great fishing day, don't you, Gordon? Let's go fishing and frog hunting," Norm asked. Many a fish were caught with safety pins.

"Get him!" yelled Gordon, as Norman stabbed the frog. "Oh, boy, my second one," Norman remarked as he moved hastily on to look for the next. "Aw, shoot, I missed that big one. Dadburn it!" Gordon shrugged. "Dad was right, these slingshots are better than the gig I use," Norman bragged.

"Let's go down to the strip pits and hunt for frogs," Lee put forward. The strip pits were formed from all the coal mining. "We can really get a lot of them at the pit," he continued. "Do you think mom and dad would care if we go to the pits?" Gordon asked. "Look! We'll tell them when we bring all the frogs back," Norm said. "Okay, but I hope we don't get in trouble." After arriving at the strip pits, they began frog hunting. "Got one!" Lee yelled, "He is a big bull frog." After an hour they had seventeen frogs and never missed a one. "Boy,

mom is going to like frying these up. There are some big ones," Gordon stated. They headed back home excitedly with their prize collection of frogs.

As the boys were walking they stumbled over something in the ground. "What you got in your hand, Mugsy?" Lee asked. "Looks like a pipe," Mugsy responded. "Look, here's a domino," Gordon outburst. After digging in the ground, they found remains of a set of dominoes and pipes the coal miners had at their cabin. The dominoes and pipes were from the cabin they lived in. In their idle time the miners smoked and played dominoes.

On other ventures the boys would set out for the woods. "I got mom's matches," Gordon called out. "We'll put them on the end of a bolt and light them and watch them explode. "That sounds like fun," exclaimed Gordon. "You bring the matches; I'll get the bolts," Lee added. Lee, Gordon, and Norman headed to the woods with the matches and bolts. "We'll let them off at the oak tree by our swimming hole. Getting them ready, they all stood back. "Look at that one go into the air," shouted Norm. "Golly, That one is going higher than all of them," shouted Gordon. "Oh gosh, mom's going to wonder what happened to her matches," Norman fretted. "Don't worry, I left her a few," shouted Gordon.

The boys were hoping to make some extra money in the summer time. The church offered to let the boys mow the cemetery. All they had was a rotary blade mower. They tried but the cemetery was too large. They just couldn't get the grass all mowed. This job fell through, just too exhausting.

Gordon damned the crick with gunnysacks and made a great swimming pool. "Gordon, let's get an old tire and hang from the tree and we can swing out over the water and jump in," Lee suggested. Norm and Gordon attached an old tire to Bess and

hauled it down to the swimming hole. Norm grabbed the tire, and Gordon helped tie the rope to the tire, and they were on the way to getting the rope around the tree limb. After a couple of hours everything was good to go. "I think this limb is strong enough," shouted Norm. So out he went. "Man! This is fun," shouted Norm. All their buddies gathered at the swimming hole and had a great time all summer long.

X. A New Tractor

The boys went to school at a one-room schoolhouse at Streamtown. Early morning before school, Gordon took his sled to school. He and his friends went sledding. "Chuck, hop on the back of my sled," shouted Gordon. They were at the top of a large hill. "Okay, Gordon, but I'm a little scared!" he commented. They both couldn't stop and ran into the creek. By the time they got to school, they were freezing. "Gordon, your clothes are so wet. We must get them dry before you catch a death of a cold," Mrs. Beasley rambled. The teacher had to put Gordon in the closet and dried his clothes on the boiler. "Your clothes are dry now, Gordon. I'll hand them to you, Gordon, and you can get dressed now," old Mrs. Beasley snarled. She really didn't like the extra work. She had taught for thirty years, and was ready to retire.

As Norman rode Gordon on the handlebars of his bicycle to the local store, here comes the neighbor bully, Jeff Traxel. They were riding straight toward each other, and playing double dare. Norman was not budging. "Move over!" Norman yelled, but Jeff kept on coming. They collided and bent Jeff's tire.

"Look old chap! I'm going to tell my dad on you!" Jeff ecstatically screamed. "Oh, go fly a kite, Jeff. You ran into me, and it's not my fault," Gordon screamed. Jeff's dad being the mayor of Covey didn't help any. This would be addressed if his dad came to the house. Seth could handle everything. He was a strong positive man. When it came to right and wrong, he would express his opinion.

Not long after, Jeff's father, Mr. Owen Traxel knocked on the door. "Hey, what's this about your boy running into my son's bike?" he blurted out. Seth went on to explain, and they sat down to a cup of coffee and started talking about politics. The incident was soon forgotten, and they became friends. "What would you like to drink, Mr. Traxel?" Sarah requested, "We have coffee, tea, or Kool Aid."

"Call me, Owen, both of you, call me Owen. I feel like good friends can go by first names," he replied. "Here are some cookies for both of you. My specialty is oatmeal, and here are a few peanut butter and sugar cookies, too," as Sarah placed the cookies on the table and muffled her way into the kitchen. Of course, with Sarah's and Seth's friendliness, the bike incident was soon forgotten.

Being water boys for local neighbors while the wheat was being threshed kept them busy. "Sarah I need to go into the store and pick up more chuck pegs. I want to get Lee, Gordon and Norman started chucking corn in the back forty. I know with their help we can get it done faster," Seth exclaimed. "Okay, Seth, but when you get back dinner will be ready, and then you and the boys can get started," Sarah responded. "I'll be back in three jerks of a dead dog's tail," he chuckled as he left.

The weeds were getting out of hand, and Seth wanted to do some clearing of fence rows. "Sarah I am going to cut weeds in the fence row with the scythe. Sure makes everything look cleaner and neater with the weeds gone, and good exercise for me. I'll be back in a couple of hours," Seth yelled as he went out the door. "Okay, Seth, we're having your favorite, chicken and dumplings tonight and fresh green beans with bacon," Sarah spoke as he left. "Don't forget the mash potatoes," he reminded. Seth grabbed the scythe from the shed, and commenced to cut weeds. He was in great physical shape, and he bragged about his 32" waistline. He loved to keep the fence rows and everything neat, and he was such a hard worker.

Jeanie and Marly loved playing outside. A spot behind the woodshed, was the favorite spot for making mud pies. After a little rain, these pies made up good. "Hey, Jeanie, what are you making?" Marly uttered. "I'm making some cherry pies and apple pies for the bazaar. We have to raise money for the hospital benefit," answered Jeanie. They loved playing make believe with the mud pies. It was so much fun as they played all afternoon just putting them on a little strip of board to dry. If the weather permitted, they would dry by the evening.

Gordon rode the ole mare, Bess, to plow the garden. "Gee," he shouted. "Haw, haw."

"Gee," brought the horse to the right. "Haw," brought the horse to the left. Gordon even made a little extra money by plowing the neighbor's garden. "Dad, I'm going over to Ms. Johnston's and plow her garden for her this evening. Is the plow ready? Gordon asked. "Okay son I greased all the bolts and I think the plow is ready to go," Seth assured. The extra money sure did help.

Plowing a small garden was three dollars and for a larger one just only five. "Move over, Bess. You're getting too close," screamed Gordon as he plowed Ms. Johnston garden, "Don't you step on those plants!" Bess never stepped on any plants ever. Ms. Johnston gave him a homemade applesauce cake when he was done. "Take this applesauce cake home with you, Gordon. Tell your mom and dad I said, "Thanks, for letting you help me. Here's a few dollars for you," Ms. Johnston offered.

"Sarah, I have a chance to purchase a John Deere tractor, plow, and a single section harrow from Mr. Adders at the farm implement store in Covey. What do you think about getting this? The price is great, just three hundred dollars for all the pieces and I can make payments," Seth inquisitively asked her. "Seth, you've been wanting this for a long time. Go ahead and see if we can get the credit," she enthusiastically answered. Seth purchased the old John Deere tractor. This tractor was heaven for plowing and discing the soil.

The neighbor, Mr. Lomax drove Seth into the implement store, and Seth drove the John Deere tractor home. All the time he was dreaming of how much easier his farm work would be. He reached the gate and said, "Whoa!" and he ran into the gate. Having horses to do all the work for so long, he had to take some time to adjust to this new machinery.

"Norman after I listen to the barn dance, you can listen to one of your westerns," Sarah said. In the evening Sarah listened to W.L.S. barn dance on the radio. This was presented by Sears, and stood for the world's largest store. She also listened to some stories on the radio. "Mom the western I want to listen to is the Lone Ranger. I am going to turn The Lone Ranger on when you are done," Norm added. Norman loved listening to Roy Rogers and Dale Evans, the Lone Ranger and Tonto, and The Fat Man Steps on the Scales. With a day in this household obviously, they were poor, but rich in many ways, and enjoying the simple things in life.

XI. Effects of the War

Times were hard, and the war had just ended. Truman was President, Because of the war, rationing of gas and sugar followed. Everyone learned to economize. Neighbors helped neighbors, taking someone to the doctor or to get groceries. Sarah being the person she was, she knew how to deal with these problems. She was a great wife, cook, seamstress, and mother. Marly always remembered how Sarah spoke of rationing and the effects of the war. She had learned to make do, and she always said, “There are so many ways to make do, when you have to.”

Sarah was very crafty. She made all the boys a cowboy shirt, pants and chaps when they were younger. She even made them hats. Taking a wire and putting around the rim made the hat brim stand out. The neighbor children were so envious of the homemade western outfits, even though some of the mother’s ordered their western cowboy outfits from the Spiegel’s catalog for them.

Sarah motioned for Norman, “Hey, Norm, I want you to go to the neighbors, the Lomax’s, and get me a cup of sugar for an open crust apple pie. I will bake three apple pies and you can take one to them, later and keep the other two for ourselves."

"Will you make some stick tights with the extra dough?" Norman stated licking his lips. Sarah always made stick tights. She rolled out the leftover dough, just add a little sugar and cinnamon, and she rolled, sliced, and baked them about twenty minutes. In the background you could hear Jeanie, "I want some stick tights too!" Many times one of the boys was sent to the neighbors for a cup of sugar or some other ingredient for baking that Sarah was out of.

"Mom, I'm hungry," whined Marly. "No, you know you will spoil your appetite if you eat now," Sarah corrected, "Dinner will be ready in an hour. You know I don't like for you to snack before your meal. You won't eat your meal if you do." Breakfast was a full course meal, dinner was a well-balanced meal, and third was supper, usually around six.

On the evening of November 1, 1952, the day was cold and wintry.

You could hear the wind howling and blowing against the window.

The potbelly stove was going full blast. The potbelly stove was purchased at an auction. The rounded bottom was much larger than the top, thus getting the name potbelly. This stove produced lots of warm heat. The stove pipe was burning red hot. There was a warm, comfortable feeling inside. You could smell the freshly baked bread and hear the meat sizzling in the kitchen.

"Seth, don't forget to empty the ashes. I know the pan is full. We have burned a lot of wood today," Sarah called. "I'll empty them after supper, Sarah. I'm filling a hole in the yard. Eventually I hope the ashes smooth the ground over," Seth answered.

Sarah yelled from the kitchen, "Marly, don't get too close to the stove pipe, or you'll singe your hair again!" She had done this in the past, and her mother knew she had better warn her again. Sarah was finishing the last minute details and ready to call them for supper. "Come and get it, Seth, supper is ready!" her voice rang as she wiped her hands on her apron. She always wore an apron. She had sewn many for herself, but this one was hand sewn by her mother.

The chicken feed that was ordered for the little chicks came in colorful cotton sacks. Sarah washed them up, and made aprons, tablecloths, and many other household articles. She even made herself some house dresses. The girls benefited from these colorful sacks. Sarah stitched up matching skirts for them.

The washbasin was in the pantry. The pantry was located adjacent to the kitchen. Sarah kept canned goods and jellies atop the washbasin. Seth would help wash their hands, and Marly remembers how he washed and wiped each finger. As Seth scrubbed and washed each finger he said, "You don't have to be rich to be clean."

Mealtime was family time. Seth led the family with grace. Seth started his prayer with sincerity, "We are gathered here today with great blessings upon us. We are appreciative of our food, and thankful for our family. As we partake of this food, let us remember our blessings and be thankful. May God bless and keep you all. Amen." Each family member had their same seating arrangement. As they passed the food, they spoke of their day.

The cat perched on the outside of the windowsill near the kitchen table. Gordon, Marly's middle brother, reached up and said, "Kitty, nice kitty, kitty," and he pressed too hard and broke the window. Luckily the window was just cracked.

Unfortunately, Gordon had to retire early. Seth said, "Your actions were not appropriate at the table or anytime. Finish your meal and go to bed."

Other mishaps occurred at the table at meal time. Another incident Norman reached for a slice of bread, and thus, knocking over Jeanie's milk. Jeanie cried and stated, "I want some more milk, Norman spilt mine." She kept on whimpering and Sarah rose from her seat, wiped up the spill and poured her some more milk. By that time, Jeanie was settled down. Seth reminded, "Be sure to pass the food and say please and thank you. We must learn manners at the table at all times." Marly put a cookie between two slices of bread, and they all laughed, so then Marly started crying. There was never a still moment at meal time.

Bath time was on the agenda next. Every Saturday night, Sarah brought in the metal tub from the wash shed. She grabbed the large bottle of baby shampoo. Seth's favorite shampoo was Prell, but for the girls she used baby shampoo. She filled the tub with water, and when the water seemed a little too cool, another kettle of hot water was poured in. "Move over, Marly darling, so you won't get burned," Sarah softly spoke as she poured the water into the metal tub. This was the night for Marly to get her bangs trimmed. As Sarah trimmed her bangs, Marly could feel the hair tickle her nose. Trimming her bangs felt so fresh. A warm bath was so cozy and comfy. She always liked to be the first to bathe in the ole metal tub, but next Saturday Jeanie was first. The girls alternated every Saturday night.

"Norman, get in here. Land sakes, the water has been ready for an hour. I put a little soap in the water, so you can have some bubbles," Sarah called out loudly. "Gee whiz, mom I just got my marbles out. I have to pick up my marbles and put them in the sack," Norman answered. The boys also alternated bathing.

First the oldest and then the youngest, as this would save any arguing. Wash time through the week consisted of hand washing in the basin in the pantry.

Sarah used a scrub board for washing clothes when she was first married. She then received a gift from her father-in-law, Noah, an old Maytag ringer washer. Noah had purchased a new washer, and told Sarah and Seth, "You can just have this one. There is still some good in this old washer." She often wondered if he got a new one just to give them a washer, and he knew we would accept the washer under those conditions. This washer was stored in the outside shed. "Seth, I sent your dad a card thanking him for my Maytag washer," Sarah remarked, "This washer has been a lifesaver for me."

"I'm glad you sent him a card. He'll know how you appreciated the gift," Seth declared. Once a week Sarah fired up the washer, powered by a gasoline motor. With the boys getting their jeans so grimy and dirty, and Seth with his dirty jeans, the new machine was a great help. This old washer saved her lots of time and hard work.

After the clothes were washed, each piece was entered through the ringer squeezing and ridding the excess water into the rinse basin. Seth constructed a clothes line out back. Sarah hung the clothes up with wooden clothespins, and usually washed and rinsed about six or seven loads, and this took most of the day to hang and dry. "Just one more load to hang up, Lee, and then we are done. Thanks so much for helping me. We did the laundry in one day. Good heavens, I can't believe we did that!" Sarah announced appreciatively. Lee always helped with the water and carrying clothes. "That's okay, mom, after I get done, I thought I would go fishing. I need to dig for some fishing worms and grub worms. I know where there are lots of night crawlers. Those grub worms are great bait, too," Lee replied.

"Mugsy, are you going with me?" Lee inquired, "I'll let you use my new fishing pole."

"Sure," Mugsy excitedly replied. After fishing for a couple of hours and not catching very many, they were ready to go home. "We don't have enough fish to keep. We'll just throw them back in. Maybe they will grow a little, and we just might catch them next time," Lee insisted.

After reading a few Tarzan comic books, Norman dug a hole and put some sticks on top. The only bad thing was that Sarah was hanging up clothes and fell in it. "All right, boys!" Sarah reprimanded, "Which one of you did this?" "I did mom but I was trying to get an animal. In my comic book, Tarzan captured animals by making these traps, covered with grass and leaves, like I did," Norm replied. "That's okay in comic books, but you can not do that in our yard," Sarah scolded, "The animal you got was me!!! I could or someone else in our family or friends could have gotten hurt! Don't you ever do that again!" Sarah scolded. "I'm sorry, mom, I didn't mean to hurt anybody," Norman answered.

The summer was fair time. The boys had saved their hunting and seed money from selling seeds along with their allowance. "I have five dollars," Norm announced, "How much do you have, Gordon?" "I plowed Ms. Johnston's garden and painted her fence so I have eight," Gordon declared. Norman couldn't wait to toss for a stuffed animal or a live fish. Once a year, the fair came to Covey. This was a big event, and there were different amusement rides, such as the merry-go-round, Ferris wheel, and the scrambler. Different booths with the baseball toss or basketball toss for ways of winning prizes. The basketball toss and the baseball pitch could usually win you a prize. Seth always liked to have his age and weight guessed, and they always guessed him younger than he was.

Arriving at the fair, the first thing Sarah spied was a picture booth. This one particular time, Jeanie would not participate to have her picture taken. “No! No! I don’t want my picture taken,” Jeanie cried. “Marly, would you have your picture taken?” Seth asked. “Now remember smile real big for daddy,” he hinted. Marly said she would. Sarah spoke with Marly softly, “Now, don’t you move, Spunky, and the photographer will snap your picture after we pull the curtain. This will only take a minute.” They pulled the curtain as she sat on the stool. Her eyes were wide, and she was scared, but she did it. The picture showed her pudgy little frightened face. The one picture of Seth and Sarah showed them smiling and so much in love!

XII. Sunday

Rushing around in the kitchen, Sarah started fixing breakfast, and Seth and the boys were doing the morning chores. When Seth had finished with the chores, he washed his hands and freshened up and said, “Move over, Sarah, and let me have that spatula. I can help fry the bacon and eggs this morning.”

“Thanks, Seth, my ear is acting up again, and I think we will have to make a trip to see Dr. Zorrick this week. I think I have inner ear infection again. Maybe he will give me some medicine to break the infection. Last time the medicine got me better fast,” Sarah commented.

This morning they were having bacon, sausage, eggs, toast, hot chocolate or coffee. Plenty of bacon, sausage, meat and eggs were always available. Usually a neighbor or family member would go halves, and everyone would butcher together a pig or calf, and split the meat. The wives would wrap the meat, and bring in the lunch for the day. Pigskins were deep-fried in the lard, and cracklings were made. The appetites were ready.

Sarah's ear was still bothering her. "Seth, I had an ear ache all night. We have to go to the doctor for some medicine. After a trip to Doctor Zorrick, she was confined to bed rest. Besides the inner ear infection, she was anemic. "Sarah, I want you to know you are required to have complete bed rest. Seth, you will have to make plans for this to happen. This lady is one overworked woman, and she must get rest. Her immune system is down, and the only way is complete, I mean complete, bed rest," Dr. Zorrick insisted. "Don't worry, doc, I will take the girls to Aunt Paula's and me and the boys can fend for ourselves. The boys can take care of their mother," Seth agreed.

Seth arranged for the girls to go to their Aunt Paula's and they would return at the end of the week. Their young cousins could help take care of them and Sarah would have time to recuperate.

"Mom, how do you make pancakes," Gordon inquired. Sarah told him, "Get the recipe book out, and there are complete instructions on the fifth page. I always use this recipe, and you all like them really well," Sarah weakly answered. "Use some of your molasses you collected from the sugar trees," Sarah suggested. Earlier in the spring, the boys had tapped the sugar trees. They boiled the sugar down and brought the contents to the house and Sarah finished boiling down for molasses.

"Gordon, will you wash a load of clothes? Separate the dark ones and the light ones. Lee will help with the water and Norm can hang them on the line. Thanks, boys!" their mother ordered, "I need to take my medicine now. I feel like I'm getting sick to my stomach," Sarah noted, "Would you bring me the bottle of aspirin on the shelf by the sink? Oh, also bring the Pepto Bismal, Norm."

The girls spent five days at Aunt Paula's where they had older cousins and by the weekend they were able to come home. Sarah was much better and on the road to recovery. The doctor warned her to go slow.

Sunday was not a working day, besides the morning and evening chores with the animals. Sunday was a time for visiting family and friends, relaxing and going to church. Getting to the church on time, Marly stayed by her daddy's side. She held his little finger as she walked by his side. Running a little late one Sunday morning, he looked down at Marly and said, "Better late than never."

One of Seth's friends, George Alyea, pinched her nose and twist her ear trying to get her to smile. Of course, Marly tried to smile as big as she could. Eulah Treckley, sitting in the front pew, sang at the top of her voice. She thought she had a beautiful voice, and her voice wasn't bad except she blared out all those favorite hymns so loud it was deafening to your ears. "Hallelujah", "Amazing Grace" and many more. She could be heard above them all.

The minister spoke, "Let's all get to know our neighbors. Just shake a hand with your friends in the pews around you, and say hello." Eulah turned around and looked at Marly and said, "Hi you little sweet thing, you are just as cute as ever. Do you want to come and sit by me?" Marly shook her head and said, "I want to sit by my daddy."

Eulah's mother, Grandma Treck, made Marly a rag doll. "Here, sweetie, I made you something. I hope you don't mind the bad stitches," Grandma Treck warbled. The doll was made from a white sock with black button eyes, pink felt hair, and a red cotton dress. The most amazing thing was that Grandma Treck was blind. There were a few crooked stitches, but Marly never even noticed. "Thank you so much, Grandma Treck, I love it very much. I will name her Anna," Marly voiced.

Seth was singing a special this morning, "The Old Rugged Cross". Seth and Sarah were being baptized after the church ceremonies. Seth had been singing since he was little. He sang many a special at the small country church he attended as a lad. As he sang this morning, Marly could hear the tone of his beautiful voice singing, "On a hill far away the old rugged cross" and the words came pouring out in a beautiful tone, "I will cherish the old rugged cross."

In the summertime was Bible School and Christian endeavor. Bible school was every weekday afternoon for two weeks. This was from two to four o'clock. In craft class, Marly painted a small plaster sheep and set this sheep atop a dresser in her room she shared with her sister. Lots of games and refreshments followed the classes.

Singing was a major part of the day also. "Okay," Norma, the choir director announced, "We're all going to sing "Deep and Wide" and don't forget the motions, but please don't hit your neighbor." Norma began leading the singing, "Deep and wide, deep and wide, there's a fountain flowing deep and wide." The children were stretching their hands and arms as wide as they could, trying to touch their neighbors, just as they were instructed not to do. Christian endeavor was a group that assembled every other Wednesday night for Bible study. Marly was fairly young to attend, but her other siblings attended faithfully.

Sunday afternoon was a time for visiting, heading over to grandma Hannah and grandpa Lyle Linzee's, Sarah's mom and dad. This was a quiet afternoon. The children were playing outside, and Marly went to the front door, knocked, rubbed her tummy and asked for one of those big sugar cookies her grandma always had in the top of her cupboard. In grandma's kitchen was an old fashioned wood burning cook stove. Lots of cooking and baking were done over the years on that old stove. "You can have one cookie, Marly, but just one because we don't want to spoil your appetite for dinner," Sarah hastily remarked. They all agreed just one cookie.

Uncle Mose sat down in the comfortable chair speaking as he sit, "Hannah, where is that new Alden's catalog I heard you say you received in the mail last week?" Hannah brought the catalog to him, "Here you go, Mose. I know how you like to shop in the catalog." He spent hours just drooling over everything he would like to buy.

Seth smoked and chat with Mose. Seth laid his head back on the soft comfortable sofa chair and napped just sitting in his chair. He fell fast asleep and he snored very loudly. When Sarah went to church, she had to kick Seth to keep him awake. Sometimes this embarrassed Sarah, because he kept falling asleep during the sermon. The monotone voice of the preacher just put him to sleep every time.

Seth and Sarah visit with the neighbors, Mr. and Mrs. Fred Lomax. His wife Maude chatted with Sarah about ladies aid, which they were both members. "Sarah what do you plan on making for the craft bazaar?" Maude asked, "I think I will crochet those small dish cloths you like so well."

"I think I'll crochet some small doilies. I can make them in no time. I guess we have a couple of months, so we should be able to make up quite a bit of crafts. I think I will also send divinity, fudge and popcorn balls," Sarah responded. Seth and Fred had a discussion about farming and the crops or the garden. Maude suggested they all play a good game of euchre. "Sounds like a good idea, don't you think so, Seth," Sarah affirmed.

The game began. Maude fixed them all a cup of coffee. "Sarah, you and Seth both take cream, right?" Maude questioned. "Sure, but sometimes Seth takes sugar also," Sarah confirmed. "Sugar and cream today, Maude, thanks," Seth responded. Seth was so polite, always thank you and please. Fred, with his gruff, raspy voice stated, "Remember, girls, Seth and I are unbeatable."

After the game began, Seth let out a roar, "I'm playing a loaner!" Fred laid his cards down. As they continued the game, Fred pulled each trick in. Seth bellowed, "Mark us up four!" Then he let out a great big chuckle. Fred laughed, "I told you we were going to be unbeatable!"

XIII. Growing Up in the Fifties

"Mom! Hey mom! Where are you?" Norm inquired, "I'm going fishing at the crick behind the barn. I have my chores done."

"Okay, but, good grief, no fishing worms or frogs in your pockets today. That was disgusting when I did the washing last week. Take your little tackle box to put your fishing equipment in," she insisted.

Growing up in the fifties, Lee, Norman, and Gordon spent a lot of time in the woods. Many an adventurous day was spent back in the acreage behind the house. With a slight gentle breeze and the full green foliage on the trees, the boys all headed to the woods with a couple of friends, each carrying their fishing poles. They dug the fishing worms and grub worms for bait, and had plenty of safety pins, hooks, and made their own bobbers out of weeds. "Today is going to be a good fishing day. The wind is out of the west. Grandpa Linzee always said if the wind was out of the west the fishing was the best, but if the wind was out of the east the fishing is the least. If the wind is out of the north, fish don't go forth, and if out of the south, bait goes into the mouth.

"Gather up some rocks to put around our fire," Gordon demanded. Seth had told the boys if you start a campfire always put rocks around the fire to keep control of the flames. Norm began gathering the rocks, and they started a fire. "I bought some bacon," Lee presented. "We'll cook us some good fried bacon. I brought some of mom's homemade bread, too," he added. After getting the fire started, one of the rocks blew up far above the trees. "That sand rock must have been full of gas," Lee added. "Mugsy, gather up more sand rocks. After we eat our bacon sandwiches, we'll hide behind a tree, and watch them explode. Let's hurry up and eat," Gordon hollered. They gobbled up their sandwiches, and they all began gathering sand rocks, and put them in a pile. Lighting a fire, they all stepped behind the biggest tree they could find. Boom! Boom! Boom! What an explosion!!! "Man, look at them," Lee exclaimed. "That was fun, but we better head home. Mom is going to wonder where we are for supper time," Mugsy declared. Away they went.

On another trip to the woods, Gordon, Norm, and Spike all headed out for some adventure. Spike shouted, "Hey, guys, let's ride a tree down!" He got the bright idea to cut down a tree after someone had climbed to the top. Boy! What a ride down! So, Gordon picked a tree without many branches. "I'll take this one!" he clamored. He climbed up to the top and held on. He came down a lot faster, and was knocked out. Lee took off to the house to tell their mom, "Mom! Mom! Something happened to Gordon! Come quick and follow me!" He thought Gordon was dead.

When Sarah and Lee arrived to the woods, Gordon had regained consciousness. "Are you okay, Gordon? Where does it hurt? Do you have any broken bones?" Sarah rambled. "I'm sore all over and I only have a cut on the bottom of my chin,"

Gordon whimpered. He was assisted to stand up by Lee. After taking him to the house, Seth had returned home from work, and Seth helped him into the old Chevy and headed to the office of Dr. Zorrick, and he received eight stitches in the bottom of his chin. "Ohh!! My head and my chin hurts, Dr. Zorrick," Gordon cried. "Look, Gordon, you had quite a bump on your head. You might have a slight concussion, but nothing a little bed rest won't help. You remember no more riding trees. You are a lucky young man. You could have injured yourself badly," he declared. The family all headed home with a little medicine and relieved things went as well as they did.

Marly and Jeanie were not very old, so they just usually played close to the house, and ran around barefoot. Living in the country was a peaceful and quiet life, but very enjoyable and relaxing, just enjoying the simple things in life.

The game of marbles was a big rage with friends at school. Sarah had stitched up some small bags for the boys to put their marbles in. Most all the boys at school had a bag of marbles attached to their belt loop. The one with the fullest sack meant he was the winner for the day. To play marbles, a large circle was marked in the dirt with a stick. Each person had a shooter marble. By knocking a marble out of the center of the circle, that marble was yours. You were a lucky person if you had some of the prettier marbles, such as the cateyes.

Most boys had pocket knives. "Spike, let's play stretch at recess," Gordon proposed. "Sounds good to me," Spike answered. When playing stretch, all the boys formed a circle. Each one had a pocket knife. The object was to make your opponent stretch so much they would fall over. The ones that fell over and lost their balance were out. Each time the knife was thrown in the ground you stretched your foot. The knife had to stick into the ground. Last man standing was the winner.

The first game narrowed to Spike and Gordon. "Spike just you and me," Gordon bragged. Gordon had to stretch and made it. "I'm out Gordon, you won. I can't stretch that far," Spike conceded.

"Mom, we're going to the woods today. John and Larry are coming over. We'll be gone all day. Can we take a little food? I thought maybe peanut butter sandwiches or baloney," Gordon announced. "Remember your chores. Did you feed the chickens, Gordon? I'll pack you some lunches," Sarah replied, "You can pick them up before you leave. I'll set them on the table."

"Sure, mom, I'll finish my chores and we'll head out to the woods.

We won't be home until this evening. We're building a fort," Gordon acknowledged.

Heading to the woods, John and Larry came along. "We'll build a log cabin, guys, or a fort, whatever you want to call it," Gordon declared. "Let's eat our lunch first, and then we can begin," ordered Gordon. After eating all began chopping and sawing trees, until finally they had enough for the frame. A few more times in the woods, they had their project completed. This was hard to believe, what they accomplished. Gordon was just a chip off the old block. Grandpa Linzee set out to do a project and he finished it.

"Spike is coming over tonight, Lee," Gordon shouted. "He told me at school today. He wants to take our dog Duster and get some watermelon. He said we can get all the watermelon we want because old man Dugger, the neighbor, is scared of Duster," Gordon continued. "Watermelon sounds good, but I don't want to get into any trouble," Lee shrieked.

XIV. Lee and the Ole Beech Tree

Lee loved hunting and trapping. He and his brothers were eager to trap and hunt, a little way to earn some money from selling the hides and have some fun. Hunting was one of the loves of their lives. Being a country boy gave them the chance to enjoy their favorite hobby. "We have to set our traps tonight," Lee ordered, "Gordon, I want you to set one trap behind the barn on the east side in the empty field. Put the trap right by the old fence post at the edge of the field. I'm hoping to get a muskrat or a beaver."

"I'll set them tonight after I go fishing. The fish are biting today. I'd like to catch that big catfish I've been watching in the stream the last two weeks," Gordon announced.

"While the boys were fishing, Seth and Sarah were working around the house. "We better look in the catalog for some warm boots this year, Seth, for you and the boys," Sarah mentioned, "With all the farm work and the boys trapping and hunting we need to keep your feet warm. At the same time we should check out boots for the girls also."

"We have a new Aldens catalog. Price them in the catalog, and I will price them at the department store in Covey," Seth emphasized.

Lee, Gordon, and Norman all went to check on their traps. "Look, Lee, we got that big muskrat we've been trying to get for the last month," Gordon announced. "Jumping leap frogs! Look how big he is!" shouted Norman. The boys trapped and sold their hides to Sears. All their trapping supplies were purchased from Sears, and all their hides were sold to Sears, a good little business for some eager boys. Sears would resell the hides to different companies wanting the fur. The coon skin cap was made from several of their hides.

When Lee got home from school, he grabbed his single barrel 12-gauge Stevens. "Mom! Mom I'll be back to help with the chores after I go squirrel hunting a while," he called out to his mother from the yard. She was hanging up clothes. "Okay, Lee, just get home before dark, and I'll need your help," she shouted back.

Lee headed out to the woods for squirrel hunting. This morning was a rather windy day and too much wind for squirrel hunting. He came to the one old hickory tree that he could always get a squirrel. Sitting his single barrel 22 gauge Stevens gun up next to the old len tree, he sat down gazing at the sky. What a peaceful place! He got out his jackknife that he had won for selling the most seeds, and began carving his name and the year delicately and carefully into the wood of the beech tree nearby. Carving his name slowly, blowing out the sawdust, finally after several evenings, the name and year was etched into the wood. Lee stood back and admired his work. He thought, "After two weeks of carving after school, I finally got the job done." He sat down by the tree nearby gazing at his work again, and fell asleep. After about an hour had lapsed, he got up and headed home. Now was time to do the chores and help mom with the kids and the work.

"Sarah, I couldn't get much sleep today. I sure will be glad when I can return to days," Seth yawned as he spoke to Sarah. Seth had a nighttime job at a steel factory a few miles away. He rode with some neighbors to work, thus Sarah was alone with the children in the evening.

"I'm home, Mom, I'll go milk the cows, and I'll be back in to help with the dishes and other chores," Lee announced as he watched his mother working away. "Thanks, Lee, the weather forecast on the radio says we are supposed to have rain tomorrow, and I need to get all the clothes off the line. If you could help with that, I would appreciate it!" Sarah replied as she kept on preparing the supper.

XV. The Fire

Seth was on the four to twelve shift at a local factory. He was not very crazy about this shift, but this was a good source of income for the family, and the only shift available. He was always ready for the weekend to come, as he also had a little bit of farming and a few animals. "This weekend, Sarah, I'll mend the fence around the barn. I should get a lot of work done. The weather is supposed to be good. No rain is expected," Seth added enthusiastically. "Don't worry, Seth, we'll try to weed the garden and plow the rows. That will be one job done.

Maybe we can get some fence painted, too," Sarah established. Weekend was a special time for the family, so working through the week was not that hard. Eventually he was hoping to get bumped up to days as a few were talking about leaving which would give him more seniority. The boys were old enough to help their mother, and everything ran rather smoothly.

One of Sarah's usual week day evenings, she was preparing the evening meal, when the French fry grease caught afire and everything started catching ablaze. "Help! Come help me!"

Sarah yelled, "Gordon, get a bucket of water. Jeanie, pump fast we need more water!" The fire became out of control very fast. The fire became very intense. The grease started flaming and blazing. Sarah screamed, "Gordon, hurry, more water and start throwing water on the fire." Gordon commenced to throw water on the fire. The fire and oil and water were all mixed.

Lee was not home. He was staying after school working on a project he was making in shop class. He loved his shop class and was able to make different pieces of furniture, such as end tables, magazine racks, whatnot shelves and other items. Working away on sanding the furniture, he never even knew the catastrophe at home.

There was nothing Sarah could do. With her inexperience with fires, she never realized or even thought she could smother the fire. Marly could have never imagined Sarah smothering the fire with one of her blankets. She was so particular with everything she owned. Later evidence showed the kerosene container for the stove had jarred loose spilling too much kerosene into the stove, thus igniting and everything turning into flames.

The previous occupants had remodeled the kitchen by adding on an extension. In doing so, the cardboard installed between the partitions caught afire. The gusts of wind made the fire worse. Had the winds not been so strong, the damage could have been kept to a minimum, but things were as they were, totally out of hand.

Marly followed Norman to the fence, and she dropped her shoe she had been polishing. Norman ran to the neighbors. Norman hysterically startled rambling, "Mr. Lomax, call, call, the fire department!" "Norman calm down, get your breath, what is wrong?" Mr. Lomax demanded. "Our house is on fire, hurry!" Norman shouted. "I'll call now, and fire trucks will be on the way!" he responded. Two or three fire engines arrived within ten minutes.

Of course, Lee still was not home. He had gone to his friend's house after shop class, and he did not know anything about the fire. Jeanie was helping Gordon pump water. The old pump in the kitchen was spurting out water as fast as they could pump. Fire was on top of the spills of water. Marly kept wondering about her new little doll with the pink dress and rollers. Was her new doll going to burn?

The fire departments could not put the fire out. The firemen tried their best, but with the savage wind that night, there was no hope. The neighbors helped to salvage a little furniture, and some albums. The pictures were falling out of the albums as they carried them. Some were damaged by the pebbles, and being stepped on. There were no clothes saved except the ones they were wearing. Friends carried out the huge stove in the living room and saved it. After the fire was over, the men were going to move the stove again, and they couldn't budge it. This incident was unexplainable.

Sarah was at the end of the lane sobbing as Marly looked on. Marly couldn't stand to see her mother cry. "Oh, dear, I'm going to lose everything. My pictures will burn," she cried. Luckily there were pictures saved, but at that moment Sarah did not know they were carried out. She could see the new electric wires that had just been installed. She could see the wires from the kitchen falling. The house burned to the ground.

The children were dispersed in different directions with family and friends. Marly and Jeanie were sent to Bob Rodgers, one of the teachers at their school. They were soon settled into the neighbor's home. "Would you girls like some ice cream?" Mrs. Anna Rodgers asked. "Okay," they shyly answered. The ice cream was so good, but that was the only good thing that night, except they were all safe. Lee, Norman, and Gordon went to their grandma and grandpa Linzee's, and Seth and Sarah stayed with his parents. They had a lot to discuss and plan. At least, all the family was safe. Sarah and Seth agreed the most important thing nobody was injured. They could always find a different house, and they could definitely make it a home.

By the time Seth had arrived, the firemen were exhausted. The chief spoke with Seth and Sarah, "It is with deep regards and regret that we were unable to save the house, and thank God you are all okay, and I'm thankful for all the help we had to salvage what we could."

Seth grabbed Sarah in his arms and hugged her, and said, "This will be a new beginning, and this is the way we have to look at it. We will pray together, and we will stay together. Remember we are all safe, and that is the most important. We really have a lot to be thankful for with our children and family okay."

XVI. A New Home

Seth and Sarah moved into a rented house about one mile north of their original home, a big yellow house with four bedrooms and an outhouse. "This is a beautiful spot for us to live. The children can go to the same school, and we can adjust to our new home," Seth convinced. "I know Seth but sometimes I think about all we lost. I must think of the positive and not the negative. I guess I will think of the things we didn't lose in the fire, especially with no one getting hurt," Sarah admitted.

Behind the yellow house in the back yard was the outhouse. Without modern conveniences yet, the outhouse consist of two seats, a large catalog (with the yellow pages missing). The yellow pages were soft, so, naturally they were used first. Inside was a pot for any evening or late night duties (especially in bad weather), always having to empty the pot the next day. The house was located on a little hill with a nice big front and back yard. A small shed was located on the side for the lawn mower and some tools.

Getting a new start was difficult. Uncle Roy initiated a

collection drive for them. He distributed jars in all of the local stores in three or four small towns around. As he entered the grocery, Value Market Place in Covey, he shouted, "Hey, Mr. O"Malley, you know the Seth and Sarah Wiley family? Well, they lost their house to a fire last week. I would like to set this collection jar in your store to try and get some donations."

"Sure, Roy, I'll try to get all I can. I know Seth and Sarah very well. They shop in here all the time. Good customers they are. With a family of five, you need a lot of groceries," Mr. O'Malley noted. Mr. O'Malley told everyone of the Wiley's house fire, and he collected quite a bit of financial support for them.

Roy gathered the jars at all the local stores, and he had done a very good job with collecting funds. He was a loud boisterous type of guy. He always made everyone laugh. He headed over to the Wiley's. He had donned a dress and a silly hat. He was carrying a toaster. He entered to the front door with his bright colorful dress on. "Is your mother and dad home, honey?" he gruffly spoke. Marly beckoned for him to sit down, and she went into the kitchen and got her parents from the kitchen.

"Seth and Sarah, here's the money I received from a collection drive for you all after the fire," Roy proudly announced. "I put several jars in the different stores in Covey, and I even put one in Alec's General Store. I sure collected quite a bit for you," he related. He gave Sarah and Seth the money, which was a great financial help and was greatly appreciated. "Thank you, Uncle Roy, won't you stay for some toast with our new toaster?" "Yeah, much abides, Roy, we can sure use this," Seth reiterated.

"Bless your peapickin hearts. I think I will stay," Uncle Roy elated. Sarah prepared toast with the new toaster. She also placed her famous homemade grape jelly in a little jar, her apple jelly, and her apple butter. She placed the honey on the table, which was given to them by their spinster neighbor, Ms. Macie Johnston. The girls even put rollers in Uncle Roy's hair that day. "How do you like your hairdo?" Jeanie demanded. They were all laughing at the same time.

Uncle Roy was married to Sarah's mother's stepsister, Aunt Tina. Uncle Roy and Aunt Tina were rich, but they only lived in their basement. Why would you live downstairs in the basement when you didn't have to? Marly could never understand this as their financial status was good. Their upstairs was beautifully and exquisitely furnished, even a baby grand piano. The rumor was that Uncle Roy did not believe in banks, so he hid his money in the bricks downstairs.

With all the clothes given to them from different neighbors around the area, Marly and Jeanie contacted lice from the scarves. Sarah put a powder and hood on their head. At night they washed their hair in a solution to help free them from the nits (the lice eggs). "Let's put another solution on your hair today," Sarah bargained, "This should do it." They were absent from school a week and a half. They did not want anyone to know they had lice, as Sarah was too proud for that. The lice could be spread to classmates. All precautions were made to prevent this.

With the incoming clothes from the house fire, it was very understandable how the girls contacted the lice. Marly learned the proper name was pediculosis, which she hoped she would never contact again. "My stars! Get in the house," Sarah cautioned, "We don't want the neighbors to know you have lice."

Lee was fortunate to receive one of the main roles in the senior play. When Lee got home from school he was cheerful and delighted as he expressed to his mom and dad, "I have the lead in the senior play. He worked hard to memorize the lines. Whenever he would be working on a project or just thinking, he would bite his tongue. The evening of the play Lee forgot one of his lines, and he started biting his tongue. He knew then and there he was not cut out for the theater.

The next month was graduation ceremonies for Lee. The boys were fitted for their new suits. "We'll go into Covey this afternoon and pick out you girls a new dress," Sarah spoke, "We have a special occasion with your brother graduating. We also will have other occasions for a new outfit. I hope you girls find something you like." Marly chose a green check with fairly large checks. "How does this look, mom? I like it," Marly asserted. Jeanie chose the same dress in navy. "We'll be twins, Marly," Jeanie suggested.

"Look, girls, I think I'll try this green dress on," Sarah admonished. The wide bolero collar was stunning for her, and she looked very stylish. She was so slim and pretty. Seth bought himself a new navy suit. "How does this shirt look, Sarah? I bought a pinstripe white and navy to go with the suit," Seth expressed. "Certainly, Seth, the shirt matches perfect. Did you shine your shoes with the new polish I bought?" Sarah declared. He was always concerned with his appearance and always looked great. "By jove, I still have my shoes to polish. Thanks a lot for reminding me, Sarah," Seth reverberated.

Seth complemented Sarah, and she never went anywhere unless she was completely ready, hair fixed, hose, and dress or skirt and blouse, and, of course, heels. She never wore pants in public. Seth bought her a red jumper, and she was conscious of wearing the bright red color, but since Seth bought the jumper for her, she wore it for him. Trying on the jumper, "Sarah looked strangely at Seth, "You don't think it is too bright, do you, Seth?" He admiringly looked at her, "All right! Sarah, you look beautiful!" and he gave her a big hug and kiss.

The first grade teacher, Mrs. Cara Schmidt, was very nice. Marly and her friends adored her as their teacher. They wrote on their papers at the end of the page, "Do you love me?" with a "yes" or "no", and she always check the "yes" box.

First grade for Marly was quite a bit challenging. The principal, Mr. Hill, had very strict rules. He even spanked Gordon for receiving a D, when Mr. Hill knew he could do better. He said, "Gordon, I know you could have done better, and I am giving you these swats so you will remember that you could do better!" Mr. Hill was tall, balding, which made him look a little scary. When he said no running that is exactly what he meant. To enforce this, there was a spanking waiting for you.

The early morning recess, a classmate, Gary Rhodes, was chasing Marly and her friends, Connie Walls and Roxie White, with a dead squirrel's foot. They ran as fast as they could. They hurried and made it to the front door and halfway up the stairs. Who do you think was at the top of the stairs? There he was, as tall and mean as ever. Mr. Hill looked down upon them with a stern stare. He with a loud boisterous voice ordered, "Stop running, now, and go to the office immediately!"

Mr. Hill designated the first grade teacher, Mrs. Cara Schmidt, to spank them. "Do you think they really need a spanking?" Mrs. Cara Schmidt urged. "These children deserve a spanking. We do follow rules. There will be no running in the halls or the stairs in our school," he stated as his bald head shined and his face turned redder by the minute. The office was adjacent to the first grade classroom. All grades were gathered around the office door. A spanking drew a lot of attention, and was a momentous occurrence. Mrs. Cara Schmidt explained, "You all know why you are getting this spanking. The rules are no running. I am only doing my job. This hurts me more than it does you. I know that you will not run in the halls and school again after this spanking." The fact that everyone was watching was what hurt the most. The girls came out sobbing as the onlookers watched on. The crowd was most embarrassing. The day was soon over.

The next few weeks went very good, until Marly couldn't make it to the bathroom in time. She thought, "I hope I make it. I know I can't run, but I have to go bad." She scurried down the first flight of stairs, remembering not to run. She made it halfway down the second set of stairs. She wet her pants. Marly started sobbing. Mrs. Cara Schmidt transported her to the furnace room. Mrs. Cara calmed, "Now don't you cry, honey. Things will be all right. Other children have not made it to the bathroom on time." Mrs. Cara dried her panties on the boiler stove. She had an odor of dried urine the rest of the day. She was asked on the bus if she wet her pants, and she said, "No way!"

Mrs. Schmidt was very sympathetic. A classmate, Terry Jones, was hungry every morning. "Please, Mrs. Schmidt, I have a tummy ache," cried Terry. The only thing Mrs. Schmidt could reason was he didn't have any food at home. She let him have toast downstairs in the cafeteria. He whined and whined and nagged so much she probably did this for relief and to know he did have some food in his tummy.

Christmas this year was a little slim. Sarah spoke sincerely, "Now you know children things are a little scarce this year, but we all will get a present. You know having the fire put us back a little. Don't be discouraged because next year will be better." The children received a small gift, and only one. The boys received a flash light, and Jeanie received a pot holder craft kit. She was making pot holders for friends and relatives for gifts. Marly received a wetting doll with a baby bottle. She loved the doll.

Recovering from the loss of their home and the fire took a toll on all of them. The one thing that never left the house was the love in the family. Seth said, "You can have a house, but you have to make it a home. Right, Sarah?" He was so proud of his family, and always wore a smile. Sarah emotionally looking at Seth and replied, "Yes, we're thankful for being together, healthy and happy."

XVII. Another Move

Getting a chance to buy a house in the country next to the grade school seemed like a good idea. After some deliberation, they decided to do just that. The house had gray siding and four bedrooms. An ideal home with a nice front and back yard, small barn and shed. "Just think, Seth, the kids will have a playground year round. Won't that be nice? They will have so much fun," Sarah excitedly exclaimed as she fluttered around doing the housework. "Yeah, we won't have to wonder where the children are. They will be in the playground a lot on their free days," Seth remarked.

The move was a good challenge for Seth. Altogether there were twenty acres. He had a new job working for the state highway mowing roadsides and odd jobs, plus he would be farming the river bottoms behind the house. This gave him plenty of time for farming on the side, the love of his life. He loved watching the crops and riding in the neighborhood and looking at the beans and corn. His land ended at the river bottoms. Trying to raise crops in the river bottoms was next to impossible. If you had a rainy season, you might as well forget it. Most of your crop could be flooded, but on a good year you could make some profit. If the crops did not flood, the corn and beans were plentiful.

Seth worried a lot about his debt and if the crops would make it. He stewed around, and he would talk to himself about all his problems and how he was going to pay all the bills, and basically stay afloat. Sarah was always there to comfort and console him. "Heavens, Seth, you got to quit stewing about your crops. What will be, will be. We'll go play cards with your brother, Abram and his wife tonight. Maybe visiting with family will get your mind off of the crops," she consoled him. She was the backbone of the family. She always was positive and very intellect. She also was the financier of the two. Things always seemed to work out. She was the stability of the family because she was so optimistic. She persisted, "Seth, for love of mike, quit your worrying. That won't help. Things are going to work out!"

Sarah listened to her favorite radio show, Selene Serent. She cooked and cleaned while listening. She was a fanatic about cleaning. "Don't walk on the kitchen floor," Sarah yelled from the dining room. Norman was just about to enter the back door to the kitchen, and he decided it best that he go around. Many times she would sweep again what Marly had just swept. "Give me the broom, Marly. You missed a spot," Sarah remarked. "Okay, mom, here's the broom," Marly motioned. Marly knew she would sweep the whole floor again.

Monday evening in the summertime, the family all went to the free show. The free show was a big event in this small town of Yates, about twenty miles south of Covey. The large screen was a big huge white sheet in an open field. Bring your own pop corn and seats and a blanket for the children or lawn chairs for them. "Mom, can John and Larry Milton go with us and spend the night? Please!" Gordon begged. "Okay, they can go, but tomorrow we have chores, so we will drop them off at their home after the show is over. John and Larry lived just out of Yates," Sarah assured them. Everyone enjoyed the show and the evening. John and Larry were dropped off at their home.

The Milton's lived in a large farm house, with a huge barn outside of Yates. Zach Milton, John and Larry's father, was a carpenter, and on the side, he raised horses, and rented them to a local park for horseback riding in the summer time. John and Larry also helped work at the park helping with the horses. As they got out of the car, each spoke of the appreciation of going with the Wiley's to the free show. "Thank you, Mr. and Mrs. Wiley for taking us to the show. We had a great time," they spoke in unison. Both boys had great manners.

Living close to the school had advantages. Walking over and playing on the merry-go-round, slides, swings, monkey bars, and maypoles were lots of fun. Jeanie and Marly had so much fun in the playground. "Can Roxie and Connie spend the night so we can go play at the school ground in the afternoon tomorrow?" Marly asked. "Okay, just make sure you and Jeanie dust and pick up your room and sweep the floor," Sarah replied.

A sunny summer afternoon Marly's brothers, Gordon and Norman, and Spike decided to enter the school through the furnace room. "Hey, Spike, let's slide down the coal shoot and enter the school," Norman suggested. "Wow! Wouldn't that be fun!" Spike replied. Since some of the girls in the class were snooty, the boys decided to play a prank on them. "Hey, Norman, do you have to pee?" Spike spoke. "Sure," Norman said. They emptied the ink bottles of the girls and added urine.

A big school bell was rung each day by two classmates designated for the week. Two were chosen in the fifth and sixth grades for this chore. It was an honor to be chosen to ring the bell. After the bell rang, the class was going to start the assignment of writing an essay. “Okay,” said Mr. Hill, “I want you to all write of your adventures over the summer or something special this year. The subject can be any topic of your choice.” About that time one of the girls, Bertha, opened her ink bottle. “Yuck!” she protested violently, “What’s that smell?” The others started opening their ink bottles, but the only ones with the problem were the snooty girls. Mr. Hill with his stern voice stated, “Which one of you was responsible for this?” Of course Gordon and Norman’s face turned bright red. It was obvious who was guilty. Later Spike confessed and explained what happened.

Of course, Seth was called to the school. “Mr. Wiley, this is Mr. Hill, the school principal. I think I need to speak with you sometime this morning if possible. Can that be possible?” Mr. Hill questioned. “I can’t make it this morning, but I can at one. How is that with you?” Seth answered. “One will be fine,” Mr. Hill replied.

Seth walked over to the school at one. “Hi, Mr. Hill, I believe you wanted to see me. What is the problem? Is there something wrong?” Seth inquired. Mr. Hill went on explain the occurrences. When Seth found out what had happened, he reprimanded the boys. They all were grounded for a month, and were assigned to janitor duties at the school for two weeks.

Lee had four coon dogs. “Hey, Chuck, let’s ride over to Barry’s and go coon hunting tonight,” Lee proposed. “Sounds good,” Chuck replied, “My coon dogs are ready to tree those coons. They are really active today, and raring to go.” The boys and their friends went coon hunting all the time. The boys had carbide lights that fit on their hats so they could see at night. The frightened coons would run up the tree, and the ole coon dogs would howl and howl. You knew then the dogs had treed a coon.

Lee and Chuck drove over and picked up Barry. "Don't forget your carbide light, Bear," said Chuck. His nickname had been Bear ever since he was little. Off they went that night into the woods. Of course, Gordon and Norman followed along. "This new coon dog I got is really good," wailed Lee, "Just listen to his bark!" About that time Duster, the big old coon dog, took off and started howling and barking. This was a howl you would never forget. "I see him!" yelled Norman, "There he goes!" "Look! There's a baby coon following him!" hollered Gordon, "O boy! Grab him if you can!" Gordon caught him and put him in their cage and away they went. This is the only coon they retrieved. They were excited.

"He's so cute. Let's pick out a name for him," Norman piped up. "Let's name him Porky," Gordon said, "He is so fat!" Porky was everything you would want in a pet. Naming him was not hard as he was a little chubby and plump. "Yeah, let's call him, Porky," said Norman, "He's so pudgy and he looks like a Porky to me." Porky fetched articles out of your pocket. He was so fun to play with, but you had to be careful, if you squeezed him too tight, he might have an accident on you. This happened to Marly a couple of times. "Yuck!" Marly cried, "Doggone, look what he did to me!" "Now go in and wash off," Jeanie coaxed. After some scrubbing and changing clothes, in a few minutes here she came again to hold Porky. Raccoons are very clean animals, and Porky washed his food. He was just so cute and cuddly.

Lee hired Marly to feed the dogs. He laid a few pennies on the table, and left her a note. The note read: Spunk, don't forget to feed the dogs and water them. Here are some pennies for you. The dog food is in the shed, and the hose is on the side of shed. Give them plenty of water. Thanks.

Marly and Jeanie ate their morning cereal, and Marly saw

the pennies and the note on the table. She ate her breakfast and headed outside. As Marly fed the dogs, she could hear their long drawn out howling and howling, their long hound dog ears, and how frisky and excited they were to be fed and watered. This was an easy job, as the feed and water were nearby.

Marly and Lee were real buddies. Everywhere he went she was right by his side. In the spring of 1955 Lee and Marly were home and Lee suggested, "Spunk, let's go look for a television. A television is the big thing now." Lee was going to buy a television he knew that for sure. Mostly every household had a radio, but few had a television.

Lee and Marly headed out to the downtown general store in Covey. Lee said, "There it is, Marly, this is the one I want." Lee purchased the television with cash, and Lee carried the television to the car. After arriving home, Lee set the television on a stand in the living room. The first televised show they were to view was boxing. The next purchase was an antenna. The bad thing about the antenna in cold weather was going outside and turning it to the station direction. One would be inside yelling, "Whoa! Turn the other way!" hoping the person outside could hear.

Not long after Lee purchased a new t.v., Clayton Herrington, the neighbor boy, would come down and stay and stay. One particular evening, Clayton had run an errand for his mother. He was bringing back some tools they had borrowed from Seth. Mr. Herrington and Seth exchanged tools ever so often. His mother had been looking for him, and she was mad. He was late. He sat down at the Wiley's and was mesmerized by the television.

Mrs. Herrington knocked on the front door. Sarah answered, "Hello, Mrs. Herrington." About that time she saw Clayton sitting watching t.v. "Clayton Herrington, you get yourself home. Me and you have got some words!" Mrs. Herrington yelled, "I apologize for his overstay. He knows better than to disobey his mother. You are going home and I have some chores for you. I'll teach you to obey your mother!"

Lee also purchased his grandpa's Ford Model A. "Dad, I've got ninety-five dollars to put on the vehicle. Could you loan me the other hundred?" Lee coaxed. "Sure, Lee, you've helped me out a lot, and we'll just call that hundred a graduation present plus all the work you have done for us."

After butchering a couple of hogs with the neighbors, Seth put two five gallon buckets of lard into the back of the car. "I want you to take this to your grandpa Noah's and one to Grandpa Linzee's, after school. On the way Lee stopped and picked up Chuck to go with him. Lee was taking some curves pretty fast. "Slow down!" Chuck screamed as he held on tightly, "This lard is going to spill and you are scaring me to death!" "Stop buggin me, Chuck, I'm driving okay," Lee yelled. About that time both five gallon buckets spilt and they ended up in a ditch. "This is going to take some explaining," Lee stated. "What are we going to tell dad?" Norman added. "We'll have to tell the truth," Lee sorrily admitted.

On the last day of school, Jeanie wore a turquoise dress, and Marly donned a pretty pink dress. Sarah purchased both dresses on sale downtown Covey. Marly's dress had a sash on each side that tied, and little pockets. As Marly was going down the slide, one of her sashes caught on top of the slide. "Oh no!" Marly started crying, "What will mom say? I've torn my dress!" Mrs. Cara, her teacher, told her, "Calm down, Marly, I'll pin it, and your mom can stitch it." She went to her desk, and found a safety pin. Mrs. Cara Schmidt was able to pin it. Sarah easily fixed the dress later.

XVIII. Rocky Bend Park

"Mom and dad, John and Larry's parents asked Norman and I to help work at Rocky Bend Park. Can we? Mrs. Milton said she would pick one of us up early on a Monday and bring us back the next night and let the other one work for two days and bring them home. We would get to help with the horses, lead the trails, and help clean the park," Gordon excitedly announced. "We will talk this over, and will think about it," Sarah added, "This does sound like a great opportunity to save some money and fun at the same time." Seth spoke up, "I think this would be all right. One can do our chores until the other gets home, and the chores will always be kept up. I can't afford for both of you to leave at the same time, but this way would work out. Sounds like a winner to me."

School was dismissed in a week, and the Milton family would be heading to the park the next week. Rocky Bend Park's entrance was filled with bright pink petunias and yellow snapdragons accented with a touch of ferns. Park benches and picnic tables were at the first pavilion. Many a family reunion had taken place here. Rocky Bend Park was known for the swinging bridge high above the Willow Creek waters. The trails were one of the most exciting features of this park. Trail three was the hardest trail, and in the middle of the trail was the big waterfalls with a bend of rocks which the name was derived.

Gordon was the first to leave for the job. As the Milton's were coming in the drive, Gordon yelled, "See ya tomorrow night, guys!" "Make sure you packed your belongings you need. You might need extra pants in case you get muddy or wet," Sarah reminded. Getting to the park Gordon was on cloud nine. He loved the woods and the environment of the outdoors. The first job was to clean the horse stalls. He then had to feed the horses and wipe them down. The evening was fun time.

Gordon, John, and Larry all went on trail three. After getting to the bend, Gordon yells, "Look at those rocks, WOW! They are huge." John spoke up, "Man! I'm glad we went on this trail. Those are some huge rocks! We better head back before it gets dark." Heading back Gordon thought how his job was major fun and a job he would not forget.

Norman was home waiting for the Milton's to pick him up. He couldn't wait. "Mom I have my clothes packed. I also took my water bottle, and I also have my compass. Anything else you think I need?" Norman asked. "Just take an extra change of clothes. I can't think of anything else. You will be so busy," Sarah said.

At six o'clock the Miltons were bringing Gordon home, Gordon hopped out and Norman hopped in the car. Norman was so excited to go. He had been waiting for an hour. After getting to the park, all slept in the tents. The next day Norman did the same jobs as Gordon, and when free time came, John asked, "Let's go ride that double bicycle." Norman said, "What are you talking about?" Larry said, "You know the bicycle built for two."

After the work was done, away they went and headed to the bicycle tent. Larry and Norman hopped on the bicycle. Norman yelled, “Slow down I’m scared. You’re going too fast. What a ride!” Norman was so tired that night. The last day of Norman’s stay, they went on the last trail in the evening. This trail was full of squirrels and lots of birds. “Look over there, a chipmunk eating a hickory nut and the squirrels are squabbling over the nut!” John yelled.

For the whole summer the boys were able to enjoy the park. When they came home, they were constantly talking and reminiscing of the fun they had.

XIX. The Last Move

The family was moving again. Abram, Seth's brother, wanted Seth to live closer to them, and he thought Seth would love farming and more acreage to farm with. Abram lived on the old home place, and this put Seth just three miles away. "You're going to love this place, Seth. The farm has lots of acreage and country space. With a big house for your family, this house will be a dream house," continued Abram. This house was a much bigger house (twelve rooms), a big white-sided home with several acres and a large barn and sheds. Dorene, Abram's wife, spoke up, "Sarah, we can get together more often for family outings. You know how we love to play euchre and beat those guys."

Moving was a hard adjustment for Marly. She said good-bye to her friends and classmates. "Let's play jump rope one last time. Roxie and Connie started twirling the rope and Marly started jumping. They all started singing, "Down in the valley, where the green grass grows. There sat Marly as sweet as a rose. Along came a boy and kissed her on the cheek. How many kisses did she get that week? (one, two, three, four)." Marly stumbled and missed. "Your turn, Connie," said Roxie and they continued. "Let's play hopscotch, too," Marly insisted. With a piece of chalk, Marly drew the squares on the sidewalk. The game of hopscotch began.

After the game of hopscotch, the time had come to depart. "Good-bye, Roxie, I'll miss you so much, and Connie I'll miss you, too," Marly whimpered. "Don't forget we're best friends," Roxie replied. "Me, too," said Connie. They promised to write, which continued for a year. Eventually the letters slacked off and diminished, as each went their own ways and new friends.

"Seth, you won't want to miss the debate between Kennedy and Nixon tonight," urged Sarah. "I'm sure hoping Kennedy wins. I think he is a very bright man and will lead our country properly and with great leadership and expertise," Seth acknowledged, "I agree with you one hundred percent. Norm proposed, "I'm going to watch American Bandstand Splish Splash party at six, and I think the debate comes on at seven. "Bobby Darin is the guest on the show tonight. Should be good!" Norman added.

After the evening meal, Jeanie and Marly tried to finish the dishes by six so they could also watch American Bandstand. "It's your turn to dry dishes, Marly," Jeanie straightforwardly announced. "Oh pooh, but you're next," Marly retaliated, "Don't forget tomorrow night is Alfred Hitchcock and Twilight Zone. I hope those shows are not as scary as the last one. Jeanie spoke up, "I hope it is scarier!"

Seth would have a landlord now, Mr. Earl Veneer, to share profits with. He was a tall, distinguished fellow. Mr. Veneer would come to the farm once every two months. "Sarah, Mr. Veneer is coming over tomorrow, and we will discuss all of the sharing profits and business procedures," Seth commented as he lay back in his chair getting ready for an afternoon nap.

"What time is he coming?" Sarah retrospect. About two o'clock Mr. Veneer said, but he said give or take a half hour," Seth affirmed.

About two fifteen the next day, there was a knock on the door. "Hello, Seth, I am glad to meet you. I'm Earl Veneer. We spoke on the phone," said Mr. Veneer, "I am anxious to speak with you."

"Same here," replied Seth. Mr. Veneer was a very educated man and his profession was an accountant. He handled all of his mother's business, which included the house Seth and Sarah were living in. Seth was with much anticipation about farming. Farming had been his life-long dream, which was better here, because the land was so much dryer than the river bottoms. He planted corn, and alternated with beans every other year.

Later he purchased several swine, raised, and fattened them out to resell. "Sarah, get the farm market at noon. I think it is time to sell the swine. I've got them fattened up and if they are a good price, now is the time," Seth connoted. Sarah turned the radio on, and turned to the station and waited to hear the market. "Seth, I have the radio tuned in to the hog market. Be sure to listen," Sarah instructed. Seth was right, and this was the time to sell. Raising swine became more profitable than farming, and was a very profitable business.

"Sarah, I see where we can get a freezer on sale at the appliance store in Covey. We could really save on groceries. With a large family like ours, this purchase would be profitable to us. Those boys are getting huge appetites," Seth suggested. "I would sure like to freeze some pies, cakes and cookies. I could even put tomato juice in the freezer and corn. I will be picking cherries and making cherry pies. Also, I have lots of rhubarb that needs to be made into pies. Sure would be handy to just bake a pie straight from the freezer. I don't know if the peach tree outback will produce some good peaches, but if the peaches are plentiful, we will have some peach pies, also," she added, "I plan on canning my tomatoes next week, and I then plan on canning more green beans. I have a lot of work ahead of me.

"Tonight we can hull the peas and break the green beans out in lawn chairs in the yard, and break them in the evening," Sarah hinted. "Yes, we'll pick them today," Seth agreed. The whole family could finish the project in one evening.

How does a jelly roll sound with my fresh grape jelly? It's been ages since I made a jelly roll."

"You're making me hungry, Sarah, sweetheart quit talking about all that good food," Seth demanded. "Which would you rather I make for you, angel food cake or a jelly roll? It's your choice," Sarah inquired. "I'll take both," Seth laughed.

One thousand chickens were purchased. Mr. Veneer ordered a huge shed built for the chickens to nest and lay eggs. "We'll have a big egg business, Seth; we might as well try everything we can," Mr. Veneer bragged. Seth washed the eggs in an egg washer, a small bucket with wire basket that swished back and forth to rinse the eggs off. The egg washer was a really neat way of cleaning the eggs and easy. A small income developed from the milk and the eggs they sold.

Seth gathered eggs, cracked one and swallowed the egg whole. "An egg a day is healthy," he would say, and down the egg would go. Other times he cracked two or three eggs and mixed them together. Adding salt and pepper, he would dip pieces of bread into the mixture.

The transition for a new school was hard. Gordon was not very happy about the move. He just had a hard time adjusting at school. His subjects filled his whole day without a study hall to catch up. "Mom," Gordon depressingly admitted, "I'm having a hard time. I have no study time. My credits I need take all the time I have. I will be studying every night." Resentment and retaliation followed for him. His credits were messed up "Don't worry, Gordon, if you get through this year, next year will be much easier for you," Sarah graciously encouraged him.

Gordon was helping with a fun drive. "Mom, I need something for the food drive. We are supposed to bring a meat dish. I signed you up to bring something. Do you have any ideas?" Gordon inquired. "I think I'll make cream chicken since you all love this recipe so much," Sarah replied. "That will be great. We are building funds for our senior trip. We have half of the funds already, and this is going to be an exciting trip.

Gordon rode to school with Tom Macey, the neighbor boy. Tom received a new black convertible for his seventeenth birthday. "Here, Tom take a bite of this. My mom can make the best cream chicken you ever tasted," Gordon bragged. Tom took a bite. "That's good, can I have another bite," Tom begged. Finally the cream chicken was gone. "Don't let anybody know we ate it, Tom, or I am in big trouble," Gordon insinuated.

The senior trip funds were reached. The trip was by bus. Getting to see the White House and all the presidential buildings was exciting. The bus trip was long and tiring. After stopping for food, Gordon ordered a pie. He was so shocked when he received the whole pie. He had ordered a pizza pie, and he had never eaten this before. "Taste this, Tom. I got the whole pie," said Gordon, "Don't you think it's good." Tom tasted the pie and ate the other half.

Gordon couldn't wait until graduation. Norman and Jeanie adjusted better than the others, even though both of them did not want to move either. Of course, Lee was out of school by now, and getting ready to wed his high school sweetheart and classmate, Rose. Moving did not make any difference to Lee, as he was looking for a job.

"Dad and mom I have a job interview tomorrow. I sure hope I get this job. I need to bring in some money and think about my future," Lee explained. "I'm glad you got the interview, son; I hope this is the job you are looking for," Seth supported. "Make sure the pay is what you expect before you accept this position," Sarah warned.

Going to a new school was taking some adjustment for Marly. One of the classmates, Willy Baker, put a piece of sticky candy on Marly's desk. He had a crush on her, and she went "Hey, what's this!" She said, "I don't want this, and gave it back to him.

Fourth grade was really difficult for Marly. Besides a new school, Marly felt sick. "Mr. Wheeling, I am feeling sick," Marly admitted. She was tired, upset stomach, and fever. Her whole body was yellow, including her eyes. Mr. Wheeling, the fourth grade teacher, comforted Marly and said, "I will call your parents to come and get you. Follow me and I will take you to the office. You can rest in the office lounge until they get here.

After a visit to the doctor, Marly was diagnosed with hepatitis, an inflammation of the liver. Doctor Zorrick took one look at Marly and clarified, "Take this girl home. Complete bed rest for her. She has to be quiet and lots of rest. Give her lots of juices, jello and broth." She was one sick little girl.

Marly lost weight, and looked very puny. Antibiotics, bed rest, good diet, and plenty of liquids were her therapy. She was absent from school for six weeks. This meant lots of catching up to do. Mr. Veneer made a trip to give her a present. He brought a painting kit, which helped to keep her busy. "Thank you, Mr. Veneer, I like this very much," she regarded. "I hope you get better, Marly, so you can get back to school," he perceived.

Mr. Veneer came to the farm, checking making sure Seth had everything he needed. He brought his friend, Owen, with him. Owen Blakely lost both legs in a auto accident. Earl Veneer walked down to the barn, and Owen would be going with him. You could see Earl and tall as ever and Owen with his wooden blocks and walking with his hands. Quite a sight!

Mr. Wheeling, fourth grade teacher, came to make a visit. Sarah had a sign in the yard, "Keep off the grass!" The wind had blown the sign over, and the sign looked as if it read, "Keep out!" Mr. Wheeling was a little reluctant to approach the house. With a little apprehension, he did. He knocked on the door and Sarah answered, "Come in, Mr. Wheeling," Marly is in the living room on the couch."

"Thank you," Mr. Wheeling said as he entered, "I thought while I was in the area, I would check on Marly. I hope she is feeling better." Mr. Wheeling was also Norman's basketball coach. He had ventured out to check on Marly and her condition. He helped her to get back in the swing of things, and soon she was caught up with her class. "Well, Marly, you are finally up with the class. You have just this one last test to go. Your scores are pretty high, considering how much school you missed," Mr. Wheeling bragged.

When the family moved, of course, Porky came also. He was allowed to venture over the farm. He wandered into the neighbor's barn, and thinking he was a wild coon, the neighbor, Mr. John Worthington, shot him. The family was upset and all grieved over the loss of their favorite animal, Porky. Marly was still home and sick in bed, and she wrote a letter to her grandparents about his death. The letter went like this:

Dear Grandma and Grandpa,

How are you? I am feeling better. Our neighbor, John Worthington, killed Porky. He was in his barn and he up and shot Porky. Mr. Wheeling come over to see me. Momy is going to make me and Jeanie some dress skirts. She is going to send and get us some blouses and some Sun. slippers. Momy is o.k. so is the rest. I am feeling better. I hope you feel okay. I am in bed.

On your birthday I get to get up. I think. We are watching the morning show on t.v. Can you read my letter, I hope so. I am saving my money to get me a doll. Momy said I could cause I never got any for Christmas. I already have 62 cents. Mom is going to make our dress skirts. I write to my friends at my old school, also. They write back. I like to write to persons I know. I'd better close and say good-bye from Marly Wiley to Grandma and Grandpa

On the same letter, Sarah added, "Marly answered your card. The kids are all home today as the teachers are grading their Semester Exams. Her teacher came to see her. She will miss a month but he said he thought she could get caught up. She acts like she feels better and eats now and the yellow is leaving her but she is just skin and bones. She can eat just certain foods. Lee will bring me over to see you some evening. I have some vegetables to bring you."

Love, Sarah

Sarah turned ill with hepatitis, also. She had worked hard taking care of Marly, and hepatitis is contagious. Same diagnosis for her followed. Everyone had to pitch in to help out.

"Dr. Zorrick, how long will I have bed rest? My family needs me," Sarah asked. "I have dismissed Marly, after examining her, she is fine. You will need the same amount of time to recover. Be patient, Sarah. You will get better soon," he assured. "Bring me a wet cloth. Can you, Jeanie? The damp cloth will make my head feel better," Sarah weakly stated as she rolled on her side. Sarah's immune system was weak, and she came down with ear infections and the flu many times. With her weak immune system, catching hepatitis was understandable. After plenty of bed rest and her medicine, she recovered.

"Mom," Jeanie yelled from the bathroom, "How do you separate the clothes?" "Just separate a pile of dark clothes, and then put in the whites or light color clothes in the washer next. You and Marly can hang them up; Today is a good day to dry clothes. They should dry fast," Sarah stated from her bedroom. The girls did as they were instructed. Both wiped the line with a damp cloth and commenced to hang clothes. After finishing the clothes, their chores were done for the afternoon.

Sarah yelled from the bedroom, "Girls I hear the rain coming down hitting my window. It's raining cats and dogs. The clothes will just have to stay up overnight. Don't worry they can dry tomorrow. Thanks for washing and hanging them anyway."

During one of Mr. Veneer's monthly visits he brought his three children. They loved the country, as they were city folks. Shane, the oldest of the three, would help Marly gather eggs. He seemed to think if there were several eggs in the nest, the hen had lain all of them. "Oh, oh, look!" yelled Shane, "Look how many eggs this hen laid." Marly had to teach him to handle the eggs carefully, as they would break. "Shane, a hen lays one egg a day, and please, be careful, the eggs are very fragile and break very easily," she commented as she lay the eggs in the basket. "Look out for the geese. We have two geese and sometimes these geese will hiss at you," Marly warned. About that time out of nowhere, the two geese were hissing. "Move back and away," Marly motioned. "Ignore them and they will go away."

There were other pets, but none like Porky. A stray dog came and the family just didn't need another dog. Gordon took him for a ride, and he came back. They named him Boomerang. Another ride he still came back, and the last time Gordon took him much further and he never returned.

"Do you remember Bulldozer?" asked Jeanie. "I had forgotten about him, but I remember he killed and ate our chickens," stated Norman. "Don't you remember? He ate a hole in the side of our garage trying to get loose," remarked Jeanie. "Yeah, he probably wanted to get to our chickens," Norm laughed, "I sure guess that is one dog we couldn't keep. Nothing like Blackie, though, he was a gentle playful dog. Too bad he got sick and died."

"Our cousins are coming over tonight, Jeanie," Marly announced, "I want to play hide and seek or handy over." In the evening after dark, all the kids played hide and seek and handy over. "Didn't we have fun?" Jeanie spoke. "Yeah, but I am exhausted," Marly added. "Let's play Red Rover before we go in," Jeanie begged, "We have enough people."

"Okay, but I'm tired," Marly whined. "Hey, we could play dodge ball," Jeanie offered. After a little arguing, dodge ball was the game they chose.

The favorite cat was Sylvester, a black and white cat just like the cartoon. This cat caused some family quarrels. The girls let the cat inside, and this did not agree with Gordon, so he would throw it out. Gordon said, "No cat in the house!" "Well, fiddle-dee-dee, I want the cat in the house," Jeanie commented. A battle began with Gordon winning.

"Gordon and I are driving over to mom and dad's. Do you

want to go with me, Marly and Jeanie?" Sarah asked. Both in unison said, "We want to go!" Arriving at grandma and grandpa Linzee's, Marly noticed her grandpa walking around the yard and edge of the woods. "What you doing, grandpa," she asked. "I'm looking for a forked stick," he said. "What for, grandpa?" Marly asked. "I'm going to witch a well," he remarked. "You are going to what? Witch a well. What's that?" Marly declared. "I'm looking for water for the neighbors. If I can find water, they pay me ten dollars. This is unexplainable but when you walk holding the prong upwards and you are over water, the prong heads downward and there is no holding back. I'll let you walk behind me, and I'll show you. Not everybody can do this. I've made a few dollars this year witching wells," Lyle explained. As Marly followed behind him, the stick was turning downward and she could not hold the stick upward. "Wow, that is unreal!" she screamed.

XX. School Days

Fifth grade was not a very exciting time. Getting adjusted to a new school and meeting a lot of new friends, Marly chummed around with Jeanie and her friends. "Mom, Mary and Diana wanted to stay overnight. Do you mind if they do?" Jeanie inquired. "Go ahead because we are going into Calesburg tomorrow anyway. They can go with us," Sarah noted. Sarah welcomed overnight guests, and many times the girls would slip outside with a blanket and camp on the ground. The ground was a really hard bed, but camping outside was so much fun, and giggling. "Goodnight everybody, don't let the bed bugs bite," Marly said. Jeanie replied, "I hope we don't have any bed bugs!"

The girls were outside and a stray dog scared the daylights out of them. "What's that noise?" said Jeanie. "I hear something, too. Wait it's coming this way!" shouted Marly. Mary spoke up and said, "It's just a dog, go back to sleep."

"No kiddin, it's just a dog. Let's go in the house," persist Marly, "I want to go in. There are too many noises out here."

"Oh, cow! let's go in. We're not going to get any sleep with

Marly whining anyway. Good grief, Marly, the dog wasn't going to hurt anybody," Jeanie urged. "Stop buggin me, guys. I want to go in," Marly complained. They gathered up their blankets and in they went.

"Let's practice our cartwheels tonight," suggested Jeanie. Mary said, "I can stand on my head. Let me show you." Mary did a perfect head stand which was amazing. Marly, Mary, Jeanie all did some cheers for the next hour. "Teams in a huddle, captain at the head, they all got together and this is what they said, "Gotta go, by golly, gotta go, Gotta fight, by golly, gotta fight, gotta win, by golly, gotta win, gotta go, fight and win!!!!" they cheered unanimously. "One more cheer tonight. We are going to do "two bits". All right, guys begin," yelled Mary. In unison they all cheered, "Two bits, four bits, six bits a dollar all for the diamonds, stand up and holler." Diamonds was the school trademark.

The following day all went shopping at Calesburg. Norm had his license and he had driven them to town. Norm just sat in the car and listened to the radio and read a magazine. Lots of Elvis Presley songs were on the radio. The music was full blast. You could hear the words of a popular song, "He took a hundred pounds of clay, and he said, "Hey, listen." About that time Norman pulled into the parking area and the girls jumped out. Mary went with Marly, and Diana and Jeanie went their way. "We'll all meet at the drugstore in one hour," Jeanie commanded, "Don't be late. We'll all have a cherry coke at the drug store when we are done shopping."

"Sounds good," Mary agreed.

Mary and Marly went to the nearest department store. "I really like your new purse, Mary," Marly complimented. "You stay right here, and I'll go get you one," she buoyantly acclaimed. Marly insisted, "NO!! I don't want one." Marly realized she was going to steal the purse and never felt the same about her friend. Marly's parents always stressed honesty, and Marly realized obviously Mary's parents had not.

"Mom, these new shoes made a blister," Marly whimpered. "Look blisters can get infected. I'll put some medicine on the blister, and we will put tape and gauze over that. I remember one of my friends was laid up for three months just because of a blister," Sarah warned, "Infection can set in if you are not careful, young lady!"

Sarah stitched up a lot of pretty clothes for her daughters. She was an excellent seamstress; so neat with every stitch. She was always working, washing and ironing to make their clothes look so pretty. "Mom, some of the girls have so many store-bought clothes." Marly commented. Sarah responded with, "Remember Marly the grass isn't always greener on the other side. Be thankful for what you have. Count your blessings."

"Mom, could I have a hula hoop?" Everyone at school has one. They are only two dollars at the five and ten. Please! Please! Please!" Marly pleaded. "I don't see why not. You girls have been helping like crazy with all the gardening and housework. We are going in to town tomorrow, and you and Jeanie both can get one," Sarah assured her. "Maybe we can get some bubblegum, too. I want to see who can blow the biggest bubble," Marly continued. "It will be me," Jeanie responded. "Will not, will not," Marly asserted. Marly and Jeanie continued bickering back and forth. "Hush, hush you girls, good grief, you're driving me crazy with all the fussing," Sarah admonished.

"Mom, while we are shopping, I want to purchase a can-can. All the girls are wearing one. A can-can fills out the skirt and makes your skirt look so full with one. "We need to get some school clothes so we will purchase one for both of you and

Jeanie," Sarah settled. "I can't wait till tomorrow," Marly excitedly answered. "I want to get a beaded collar to go with my sweaters," Jeanie suggested. "Mary has one and she can wear all her sweaters with it," Marly added. Both girls were so proud of their new can-cans. They were trying them on under their skirts and twirling round and round. "I can't wait to wear mine tomorrow," Jeanie said. "I know, me too," Marly answered.

Marly woke up and thought, "I'd better catch up on my diary. I am a month behind." She had received her diary the Christmas before. Writing every day was quite a challenge. She opened the diary, and lo and behold there was a message in it. Jeanie had decided to snoop and read in the diary.

"Well, I'll be doggone, my sister has been in my diary, again. Jeanie wrote, "Yes, I was here, and I am a brat." The next transcription Marly wrote went like this, "Dear Diary, I will find a better place to hide you to keep my sister from reading my notes."

"Saturday afternoon I will challenge anyone to a ping pong match," Norm replied. He began to perch the net on the dining room table. Gordon stipulated, "I am first and will be the final winner. I will guarantee you. I will win!" "Oh piffle, don't bet on that," Jeanie declared.

The game began. "Go, Norm, go. You can beat him," coaxed Marly. Gordon won by a point. "Man, that was a good match, but I'm still champ!" Gordon bragged. "Cool down time, guys, I made some orange Kool Aid popsicles," Jeanie offered. "Mmmm, sounds good," Gordon replied, "Thanks."

"How about I make some homemade ice cream this afternoon? After dinner be sure to save some room!" Sarah announced. "Will you make some chocolate syrup to go with the ice cream, mom? Jeanie begged. "Sure I will, and I even have a fresh blackberry pie I will bake to go with the ice cream. I froze several with our last picking of blackberries. Doesn't that sound good?" she asked.

"On a sunny day sitting on the front porch, watching the cars go by, and enjoying the homemade ice cream, what more could a person ask for?" Seth buoyantly announced. "Yes, a perfect day! How do you like my new recipe? I used three eggs this time, and I think the ice cream has a better flavor and a little more solid. Don't you?" Sarah inquired. "Mom, this is the best I have ever eatin?" Marly gladly replied, " Mmmmmm!" "Yes, this ice cream is better, Seth. I never used junkets this time. I think this recipe is the best," Sarah mentioned as she took a bite of ice cream.

Seth ate his ice cream and went inside and retrieved his pipe. He brought out his pipe and relaxed and puffed away. "What a beautiful day!" he remarked, "This is the life of Riley."

"Life of Riley" was an expression from an early t.v. show. "No, I mean the Life of Wiley," Seth restated and chuckled.

On a Sunday morning, Seth suggested "How about visiting Mrs. Macie Johnston today after church and dinner?" "I made ham salad and potato salad for lunch. For dessert we'll have the jello I made with fruit cocktail," Sarah added. So in the real hot heat of a summer afternoon, they all went visiting to their spinster neighbor friend, Ms. Macie Johnston.

"I brought out my antique binoculars. I know you children love looking at these beautiful views through these binoculars," Macie spoke reiterating every sentence. "I remember when your brother, Lee, sat for a whole hour looking through these slides," she added. She always let the children look through her antique viewing binoculars, as they loved looking through the slides.

"My dog Spot had four puppies. How would you like one of

the puppies? They are all white with a couple of black spots. They are part cocker spaniel," Macie input. Macie was hoping to have one less puppy by the end of the day. "Well, we don't have a dog right now. We do have the coon dogs, but no dog for the girls. What do you think, Sarah?" Seth voiced. "If we take a dog, the girls will be the ones to make sure the dog is fed and watered," Sarah specified. "We will, we will," the girls spoke in unison.

The same afternoon all of them drove to the local swimming pool. Seth and Sarah watched the girls swim. The dog got sick going home and Marly couldn't wait to get home. "Hurry, dad, he is going to get sick again. I think he is car sick," snarled Marly. She wanted a dog, but this part she did not care for. Later, Seth, realizing the dog had worms, gave him some worm medicine and the dog recovered fast.

"Mom, can Rochele stay all night tonight? She lives just a couple of miles away; We could take her home Saturday morning," questioned Marly. Little did Marly know that Rochele had a bladder problem. In the middle of the night, they all woke up. "Mom, we're all wet. Yuck, come and help us?" Jeanie and Marly yelled. Sarah rose and got fresh sheets and tried to hush the girls, "Now look girls Rochele just couldn't make it to the bathroom, now you are all dry just go back to sleep." The next morning at nine Rochele was taken home. Sarah let the girls have company overnight many a night, but none had turned out as uncomfortable as this time.

Sarah heard the phone ring and answered, "Hello, this is Sarah speaking."

"Sarah, I am sorry that I have to bring you the news, but your sister Paula has passed away," Unce Mose sadly announced. For a moment Sarah was startled, but then she knew with the cancer, there had not been much hope. The last time they had visited, she was very weak and tired. "I am so sorry to hear this," she responded, "Please let me know when the visitation and funeral will take place. If there is anything we can do to help, please let us know." The loss of Sarah's sister, Paula, was hard for Sarah and the family. Paula had suffered with her illness, and now her suffering was over.

The sixth grade became challenging for Marly. The teacher, Mrs. Erlene Maddis, wanted everyone to write an essay on the subject that was of their interest. Mrs. Maddis spoke softly, "Children, I want you to write your hearts out. Write something that will catch our interest and we will want to hear what you have to say." Marly thought a while and her mind started drifting, "I know what I will write about. I can't wait to put my thoughts onto paper. All were busy writing for the next two hours. This was an easy task for Marly, as her ambition was to become an author some day. Her mind started wandering and soon she was writing away. "Okay, class, please pass your essays to the end of the row, and Max you can collect them and bring them to me," Mrs. Maddis instructed, "Clear your desk. The bell will ring in five minutes, and we will all head home." Max was her favorite student, so he was asked to pass papers, pick up the papers etc.

The next day the teacher, Mrs. Maddis announced, "I want you all to know what a good job you have all done with this assignment." She wanted to read some of them, but she decided to let the pupils read their own. Immediately Penny Maxfield raised her hand. "May I read mine first?" she stated. Mrs. Maddis said, "No, I would like for Marly Wiley to read hers first." Marly stood up. The pride Marly felt as she read her essay. She read with much clarity, as this was her best attribute. The title of her essay was, "Imaginary Minds", which spoke of going anywhere and accomplishing almost all of your feats with imagination. Imagination and dreaming can take you on an airplane or on a beach at any time. Later on in years, Marly captured this essay in a poem. This poem sums up the contents of her essay that day.

IMAGINARY MINDS

A daydream can take us on a trip,
Aboard a plane, a bus, or a ship.

When I'm alone and think of the things I'd like to do,
And try to imagine what it would be,

Of going on an ocean cruise with that special someone,
a time to dance, a time to have fun.

I can imagine relaxing at the beach,
With all reality out of reach.

I dream of flying in the sky,
above the billowy clouds so high,

I think of many things I might be,
of many professions I might pursue,

If all these dreams should come true,
think of all the things I could do.

XXI. Piano Lessons

A piano was given to the family by Seth's sister, Aunt Tiera Coats. She was Seth's one and only sister. The piano had been in the family for several years. Seth's great grandmother had purchased this piano at an auction. The piano was a huge upright piano that was very heavy to move. Tiera was taught to play classical music only. Aunt Tiera spoke with the girls, "Now, girls, you have to practice, and don't you forget it. You've heard the saying, "Practice makes perfect, haven't you? Good luck to the both of you and I hope you can get some use out of this piano. This piano has lots of memories for me."

"Thank you Aunt Tiera, we will sure try," Jeanie and Marly said in unison. The girls, Marly and Jeanie, began piano lessons that very summer.

Sarah was looking for a piano teacher for her children. Diana informed her of a great piano and voice teacher, Mrs. Alva Johns. She was well known in the area. She had about ten piano students and was willing to take on two more. After a few telephone calls, Sarah set up their first lesson.

Their teacher, Mrs. Alva Johns, was a large woman, big

robust, sophisticated lady. Her house smelt of antique furniture. "Come on in, girls, I am glad to meet you. Our lessons will be a half hour every Friday," Mrs. Johns motioned, "You can call me, Mrs. Johns, and what are your names?" "My name is Marly," Marly responded. "My name is Jeanie and I am the oldest," Jeanie added. Mrs. Johns taught piano lessons to them for a year, while Seth or Gordon waited in the car.

Going on this journey to the country was a very long drive. Seth was a slow driver, and when Sarah rode along, they both would look and compare crops. "Oh!!! Look at those beans, Seth!" Sarah would exclaim. Seth remarked, "I hope mine do that well. I hope the frost doesn't get them. I planted the beans after the hay, so they are a late crop. That's a gamble a farmer takes, I guess. Anyway, I don't have much to lose, just a few dollars for the seed."

Mrs. Johns also taught them to play duets. Playing a duet was very frustrating for Marly. "Do we have to play duets? I am not very good at this," Marly insisted. "Remember girls, practice makes perfect," Mrs. Johns assured them.

"Girls we are going to have a recital. We will get started on learning our pieces now," Mrs. Johns excitedly announced. The big recital was at an orphanage. She went on to explain, "This orphanage is for children who are not as fortunate as you, to have a home, and mom and dad to tuck them in at night. They will look forward to you coming and playing the piano."

The following week on a Friday afternoon, Mrs. Johns arrived to pick Marly and Jeanie up at ten o'clock sharp. After arriving at the orphanage, the building seemed so big. The piano seemed huge, but actually there was not any size difference. The piano was actually smaller, but being a baby grand piano made this piano look unusually big. Marly had never performed in public, and she froze. She was very shy, and blushed easily. She just couldn't think of any notes, and her stomach curled in knots. She had memorized her recital piece, but you would have thought she had never played the piano in her life. Mrs. Johns urged Marly to participate. "Now, Marly, come and play your recital piece. Just relax. All of these children are your friends," compelled Mrs. Johns, "Just like we rehearsed last week."

"Mrs. Johns, I don't feel good," Marly admitted. She had worked herself up until she had a queasy stomach feeling. Marly just couldn't get the courage to play.

At the orphanage many children were of different ages. Marly thought, "How sad to not have parents like hers with no mommy to tuck them in at night, and no daddy to hug them and say good night." She was very sad for them, and at the same time very glad for her family.

After the recital, Mrs. Johns drove to a fancy restaurant, The Family Dining Restaurant. The waitress walked over to their table and noted the special, "We have meatloaf, mashed potatoes, and green beans or you can have country fried steak for $2.95."

"Is meatloaf okay with you girls?" Mrs. Johns inquired. "I love meatloaf!" Marly responded. "Me, too," Jeanie added. "We'll have pie for dessert. There's a list of pies we can choose from," Mrs. Johns spoke as she rambled on. As they enjoyed their meal they all had a piece of fresh blackberry pie topped with a dip of vanilla ice cream.

Marly would soon learn the meaning of a tip. Mrs. Johns explained, "This is a reward to the waitress for such good service. You figure ten per cent of the bill," she said as she left the money on the table. Marly was impressed and would always remember this special day.

Mrs. Johns drove up the Wiley's long lane and as she drove

she spoke, "I am so glad you girls had the chance to participate in our recital. This was a pleasure spending the day with you."

"Thank you, Mrs. Johns," Jeanie said. "Thank you for taking us and thank you for the meal at the restaurant," Marly repeated, "We had a great time!"

XXII. Guinea Pig

Seth and Sarah loved their new home. A big twelve room farm house was just the thing for their family. Seth loved the outdoors and farming. They became friends with their new neighbors, Lynn and Bryce Stevens. Their daughter, Diana, was the same age as Jeanie, and there were two smaller children.

The old time telephone was on the wall. The Wiley's ring was four short rings. If you heard three rings, you knew the Stevens were on the phone. "Come and listen, Marly. Diana is talking to her boyfriend. Heee!," said Jeanie. "Let me hear," Marly mentioned as she scurried over to hear. "I think someone is listening and they had better hang up," Diana gruffly spoke. Many of the neighbors eavesdropped. You better be quiet or the other person would know you were eavesdropping. Oh! The things you could find out.

The phone rang the usual four short rings. Sarah answered, "Hello, this is Sarah."

"Hi, Sarah, how would you and Seth and the girls like to spend Saturday with us? We are going to the State Fair," Lynn

Stevens inquired. “I’m sure Seth would love to go. He has been talking about looking at all the new farm equipment there. We went last year and had a great time,” Sarah replied.

They all packed into one car and headed to the state fair. “Girls, you can go roam around all the tents and crafts, we will meet at the tent at three this afternoon,” Seth instructed. “Here is five dollars for each of you, and make the money last,” Sarah coached. Marly was so excited after she purchased her purple pop-it-beads. Pop-it-beads were all the rage. “Jeanie, look at my bracelet. I can have any size necklace with these pop-it-beads or I can have a couple of bracelets,” Marly proudly announced. “I wish I had gotten pop-it-beads,” Jeanie sadly remarked.

While at the fair Seth and Bryce went in a tent (a girly show). Sarah looked at Lynn and started laughing, “Let’s follow and sit behind them. They don’t know we are following them.”

“Okay, that sounds like a good idea,” Lynn said, laughing at the same time. “Look at Bryce and Seth,” Lynn declared. “Now wouldn’t that cook your goose. Look at their faces!” Sarah replied sharply. Watching the guys was best thing of the day. The women laughed and laughed because they had been so sneaky. Never had Sarah laughed so hard. Seth just happened to turn around, saw the ladies, and spoke, “What are you girls doing here? Spying on us, huh? Well, you got us, didn’t you?” Bryce said and started laughing also. After a wonderful day at the fair, all went home tired and exhausted.

The next week Norm was in the yard working on a bicycle tire, when Bryce drove up. “Norm, you’re the fellow I am looking for. I was wondering if I could get you to help me on the farm. I need some help finishing the plowing on some of my acreage. I also need some help later this year with baling hay. I know you will help your dad, but if there is some time when you are not helping him, I pay two cents a bale or sometimes I pay by the hour, a dollar an hour. "Pay was based on the distance from the field to the barn. If the distance to the barn was a far jaunt, the farmer paid by the bale. "You can start right away if you are interested," Bryce suggested. "Sure, I need a job. I was thinking about saving for a car," Norman replied. Norman began working for Bryce the next day. He had all summer to save for a car.

While he was plowing, Norman saw a big buck with antlers. He was so excited. He went to the house to tell Bryce. "Bryce there is a big buck west of your field. You need to come and see it," Norm yelled. "Norm by the time I get over there, the buck will be gone," Bryce answered. Norman walked back to the tractor and resumed his plowing and would never forget the experience of seeing the big buck.

"Dad, Mr. Stevens is putting an electric fence up to keep his cows in the pasture. This is really neat. It's just one wire around the lot. When the cows get shocked, they know they won't get near that wire. He said he may even make a lot for his two dogs. You know those Labradors he bought," Norman added. "Son, what next? I've heard of everything now. One wire keeping those animals in, and I think of all the fence I have built. What if they get spoofed or something? I don't think that little wire will take care of that," Seth rambled, "What are they going to invent next?"

Later on in the fall, Norman was able to pick out the car he wanted. He found a black convertible at the "Molton's Best Deal" car lot in Covey. He told his parents, "Look at the car before you get your groceries."

"Ok, we'll do that son, but I have to hurry and get back and water the animals. This hot weather they have to have their water," Seth stated as he headed to his car.

"We'll surprise Norm and look at the car he is interested in,"

Seth suggested. Driving in to town, as they neared the "Molton's Best Deal" car lot, they could see the convertible. "Sarah, that's the convertible at the end of the row. Wow! Look at the paint job! This car is in good shape, and I think he needs to consider checking this vehicle out," Seth opinionated. "Look's good to me, Seth," Sarah voiced.

After they returned home, Seth started carrying in the groceries, with the end of a banana in his mouth. Grabbing a banana was part of carrying in the groceries for Seth. "You know Norman that is a pretty nice looking convertible. I think you had better go see what they want for it," as Seth chomped on his banana. "I am glad you like the car, too. I have already checked the engine and the tires," Norman assured.

After going in to town, he purchased the fifty-nine convertible for $900 cash and he had one hundred dollars left for license and insurance. "Norm, I'm catching a ride to school with you on Monday, don't forget me," Tom called out Friday as they left school. Friends wanted to ride to school with Norman in his new Ford.

"Dad I'm going to have to put a little work on my car. The generator is not working right, and I need a couple new tires." Having his own car sure helped out a lot. Several of his friends bummed a ride to school from him. Norman had many friends.

Sitting in the living room, Seth was watching the evening news, his favorite time of the day. "Seth, get the door. I hear somebody knocking," Sarah called from the kitchen. Seth rose and opened the door, "Hello, I am Ted Byers and this is my cousin, Justin. We have some car trouble and I think we might have to call for some help. We are from Florida and we are headed to Chicago to visit some friends. Can we use your phone?" Ted spoke. "Sure, come on in. It is late. Why don't you call tomorrow morning? You can sleep upstairs in our spare room, and Sarah can make you breakfast tomorrow, and you then can be on your way." Seth offered. "Gosh, you really mean it. We have driven for hours, and we are so tired," Justin replied.

On Saturday morning Sarah rose and fried some bacon and eggs. Seth called, "Your breakfast is ready boys. You better get started. You need to make some calls. Ted and Justin came down stairs and gobbled their breakfast. They were starved and commented, "This is the best breakfast we have had since our trip." After their car was fixed, the boys responded, "Thanks and we will never forget your help."

A couple months later, a carton of oranges was shipped to the house with a big thank you note attached which read, "We'll will never forget your hospitality. You definitely are an inspiration for all. Signed, Justin and Ted

"Get the phone, Jeanie, will you? Sarah motioned. Sarah was just finishing the ironing and pressing the girls' clothes, making them look so pretty. "Hey, mom, Lynn wants to know if we can come over on Saturday night for euchre," Jeanie replied. "Tell her I will get with Seth, but I am sure we can," Sarah responded. The families spent many a week end playing cards.

After speaking with Seth, Sarah decided to give Lynn a call. "Hi, Lynn this is Sarah. We'll be over Saturday evening. Seth said he will get his work done by five, and we should be over after that.

Sarah brought her homemade brownies and a few oatmeal, peanut butter, and chocolate chip cookies to snack on. The grownups were playing cards at the kitchen table, and the children were gathered in the living room.

Diana went into the kitchen. She decided to make a concoction of spices and everything else, and dared one of them to drink the mixture. "Okay, who's going to drink this? Diana spoke as she held the glass. As usual, Marly said she would. She drank the mixture in one big gulp. "Good grief, I'm sick. I think I am going to throw up," Marly warbled, "I need a waste basket or something." The others were in trouble.

"My stars, what did you mix up and let her drink?" Bryce demanded. "Nothing dad," Diana anxiously replied. "My eye, you know what you put in that drink? Did you put a mixture of kitchen spices?" Bryce angrily asked. "Yes, dad," Diana cried. "Tell her you are sorry and go to bed and stay in your room!" Bryce announced. Diana was always getting into trouble. Trouble just seemed to follow her.

Diana, Jeanie, and Marly set out for a trip into the woods. Late in April was a good time for mushrooming, and extra warm for April. They began getting a little warm and came upon a crick. "Let's go wading in the water. I'm hot," said Diana. "Yeah, that sounds like fun," Jeanie agreed. Marly was unsure, but she always followed along, being naïve as she was. They started splashing and having fun. Jeanie jumped out, "Get them off me! Help! Help!" Leeches were all over her back. Diana yelled, "One's on my leg! OOOOh! Let's get out of here!" Marly jumped out so fast, and checked for leeches. "Something is in my hair," Marly screamed. "Let me look," Jeanie consoled her, "It's a tick! I'll pull the tick out of your hair, just hold on a minute." She carefully removed the tick and on they went.

"Look over there!" coached Diana, "A whole mound of mushrooms. I'm taking them home to my mom." She took off her outer blouse, and used the blouse to hold the mushrooms." They headed home and dried off as they walked.

A few weeks later the girls purchased some ammonia for their hair. Putting one blonde streak in their hair, they thought was a good idea. Of course, Marly was the first to volunteer. "Come on, Marly, you go first," coaxed Diana. "Okay, I will, but you're next," said Marly. "I will, no kiddin, I will," Jeanie cajoled. Each girl had a stripe in her hair. At school they became the center of attention.

The telephone rang the usual four short rings. "Hello," Sarah answered. "This is your neighbor, Lynn," Lynn replied, "Can your girls go with Diana and I to the drive-in movie tonight?" Lynn headed out with all the children to the drive-in movies. "Marly, you and Diana get in the trunk, and we will hide Lorie, Diana's little sister, under Jeanie's skirt," Lynn voiced. Lynn would hide a few under the skirts and in the trunk of the car. She drove to the back and let them out. She had plenty of money, but this was just a daring stunt for her. "This time, girls, if the speaker does not work good, we are going to drive to the next speaker," Lynn insisted.

Sarah and Diana spoke often of taking a small trip together with the families. So off the Wiley's and the Stevens went on a trip to the Dunes State Park in Michigan. Sarah about had a heart attack when she watched the waves hit the girls. Since Sarah was scared of the water and could not swim, this was about all she could take. Of course, the girls could not swim, and Sarah knew this. She couldn't wait to go home. One of the worse days of her life, but the girls had a blast.

Getting off the bus, Norman loved to listen and watch the American Bandstand. Every evening after school, Norman, Jeanie and Marly couldn't wait to watch the show. "Elvis is on tonight," Norman announced. Elvis Presley was popular, and everyone loved his songs. Norman was faithful to watch this show.

All the girls in Marly's class were learning the new dance, The Hop. Marly was shy, so she just watched. "Jeanie, the newest dance is the mash potato. I think I can do the mash potato. Can you?" Marly quizzed. "I can sure give it a try," Jeanie cried out as she started swaying and twisting her feet.

A gas station was one-fourth mile north of the Wiley's. The boys called this station, "Hey, Carl, do you have Prince Albert in the can?" When the manager said "Yes", the boys said, "You better let him out!" and hang up and start laughing. The girls walked to the gas station for an ice cream sandwich many times. When Marly was younger she stopped at the gas station with her dad. "Would you like a coke, Marly?" Seth inquired. "Yes, thank you, daddy," she replied. This was her first coke. The station had the old-fashioned coke machine with water, and a slide lid dispenser. "We better get home, Spunky, I want to get my chores done so I can watch the Red Skeleton show," Seth declared. "Last week his show was hilarious," he included. "Yeah, dad, I remembered how you laughed and laughed at his jokes last week," Spunk responded.

XXIII. Toronado on Easter Sunday

"Sarah did you lay out my clothes and press my shirt?" Seth asked. The family was rushing around getting their Easter clothes on. Sarah had sewn new dresses for the girls. They were identical except Marly's was green and Jeanie's was turquoise. Each dress was so precise with the seams and the style was perfect for their slender figures. The boys were fighting over the brush and comb, and trying to look their best for Easter Sunday.

"Today is the first Sunday for our new minister, Mr. Ryan. I hope he is a good speaker," Sarah mentioned. "I guess he originally was a minister from another small church in Illinois, so he would definitely fit in with our small church," Seth added, "I am excited to hear him speak, and I hope he likes our church. I guess Mr. Ryan and his family plan on moving into the parsonage. I know the family will like our school district for their children."

"When we get back, we'll have pork chops, mashed potatoes, and applesauce for our dinner. I can fix this meal in no time. After dinner and our food settles, we'll all have a good game of badminton," Sarah spoke. "Are you going to play, dad?" Norman asked. "Why sure! I'll beat you all," Seth bragged. "I'm going to play, too," Sarah announced, "I'm pretty good, myself."

"I'll set the badminton net up when I get home," Norman optioned. We have about four birdies, so if we lose one, we still have plenty."

"Yeah, and no spiking the birdies. That is cheating. Us girls aren't that fast," Jeanie added.

After the church services and the dinner were over, the family rested for awhile, and the girls did the dishes. In the afternoon the big badminton challenge began. Seth, Norman, Jeanie, and Marly challenged Sarah, Gordon, Lee and his high school sweetheart, Rose. What a match! The birdie was swishing fast, and the score was tied. For the final point, Jeanie hit the birdie across the net, and Norman missed by an inch. "Dagburnit, I missed it," Norman shouted. "We won! We won!," the girls started screaming. "We'll play the best out of three matches," Seth stated. After the matches, all were tired.

"Look's like the clouds are getting dark, and a slight stillness in the air. I've seen clouds like this before. I think a storm's abrewing," Seth voiced, "I heard the forecast on t.v., and we are supposed to have some storms."

"I think you are right. You kids pick up the badminton rackets, and put the net away. If this keeps up, we will all have to go to the root cellar until the storm subsides," Sarah coaxed.

"Hurry, everyone get to the cellar. The wind is getting pretty strong. You know the small shed we store tools in. The wind has already picked up the shed and I see parts all over the yard," Seth yelled. "Oh my goodness, come on kids, let's hurry. The family went to the basement, and set the storm out. Norman brought his book to read and a flashlight, and the girls with their little flash lights played cards. Sarah and Seth chitchat about farming, and all their projects. Soon the storm was over. All came up from the basement, and resumed their day.

The Stevens invited Seth and Sarah for a Sunday drive. "We're going to drive over to Lexin, about thirty miles from here. I guess the tornado really did some damage. The girls are going to stay home and play games, and just lounge," Lynn mentioned. "Sure we would like to go. I have never seen the aftermath of a tornado," Sarah said.

After arriving and driving into Lexin, Bryce decided to park the car and they all got out of the car and walked around the town. "Look over there! The house is completely gone. I see pieces of a bed in a tree," Bryce noticed. A young man standing by the scene spoke, "Yeah, the mom and dad and their two children survived in this house. Believe it or not! They all huddled in the southwest corner of their basement. They are all here to tell about it. I am their neighbor and my house is over there. Never touched my house. See the debris spread out over there. That was a trailer. One child is missing and the parents didn't make it. By geminy, those tornadoes are mean, I mean real mean. Mighty strong winds, they are. From the basement I saw the neighbors' chickens twirling around and flying in the air. Quite a sight! Head for safety if one comes your way. I stayed in my basement until I didn't hear anything or any wind. Sounds like a train, you know. Real scary, real scary, it is! I'm still having nightmares."

"Look at the car wrapped around the telephone pole. Looks like pieces of straw ran through the pole. Wow! I can't believe this. I guess we were lucky this storm didn't hit our area. Sure is hard looking at this devastation. I feel for these people. I guess we need to say a prayer for all the families and the loss of their loved ones, and hope the community gets settled again,"

Seth sincerely spoke. Lynn added, "Looks like to me you can see the path wiped out by the tornado. Some houses standing and the ones in the path are flattened." Sarah said, "We are lucky that we have never had a tornado, yes, we are so lucky."

XXIV. The New Neighbors

"We are going to have some new neighbors, Seth, Mrs. Oma Huxton," Sarah noted. "How did you find this out?" Seth queried. "Lynn Stevens told me. Mrs. Huxton is a sister to Mr. John Worthington. Oma Huxton and her two boys, Zane and Wade, will be moving in next week. You mean, Mr. John Worthington that shot Porky? Seth asked. "Yes, I guess Mrs. Huxton is an accomplished pianist. We will invite them over. The girls would love to hear her play. The boys can play some board games with the children," Sarah replied. "New neighbors sounds great, and we'll make them welcome," Seth beamed.

A couple of months later, Sarah made some pineapple upside down cake and lemonade and invited the new neighbors over. "Come on in, Mrs. Huxton," Sarah amicably motioned. Mrs. Huxton entered, and introduced her two boys. "Thank you for having us over. A nice gesture it was," Mrs. Huxton replied, "I bought some music to play for you and your family." After a short visit, they all went to the piano. Mrs. Huxton could make that piano talk. "Wow! Mrs. Huxton, you are quite good," Marly responded. "My next piece is a chariot race "Ben Hurr

Chariott Race" and I made a copy for you. Remember with piano practice makes perfect," she reacted," I hoped you would like this piece. It is quite lively!" "Thanks for the music. We'll get started on it right away," Jeanie asserted. The piece was complicated, but with lots of practice and memorizing, both were to make some progress.

While Sarah and Mrs. Huxton visit, Marly and Jeanie brought out a couple of board games. "Which would you rather play? I have Scrabble or Parcheezi. We could also play card games, such as crazy eight or war," Marly motioned as she pointed to each game. Oh, I also have aggravation."

"I think aggravation," Zane replied. Wade goes, "It's my turn first."

"No, I'm first," Zane replied. "Look, to be fair we will draw for who goes first," Marly insisted. After rolling the dice, Wade went first. "You jumped a place, and you cheated," Zane accused Wade. Immediately a fight began. The boys started quarreling. Mrs. Huxton ordered, "Boys, we must go home. Quit your fighting now. Thank you for your hospitality and I apologize for the misbehavior. Tell Mrs. Wiley you are sorry, now."

"We're sorry," they both stated in unison.

After that experience, Sarah decided maybe they had better keep their distance. The boys did seem a little competitive and troubled. "Sarah, we want our children to share and manners, so we will not be able to associate with ones who do not value this," Seth commanded. "Birds of a feather flock together, and we can not be a part of their actions. Our children will learn sharing, caring, and manners. We can not allow these boys attitude in our home," he declared, "and these actions are not improving or changing. We will not tolerate misbehavior in our household."

XXV. Tragedy

"Hurry, there's some fighting over at the neighbors, dad," shouted Gordon, "Mrs. Huxton's boys are at it again. All they do is fight." Seth shouted to Sarah, "You better call the police. I've got a feeling we may need them. These boys are always fighting and act as they hate each other. Call Mr. Worthington, too. His phone number is on the pad hanging on the nail by the phone. I think his ring is five short rings." Sarah ran over to the phone pad, and checked the number and picked up the phone. She dialed five short rings and spoke with Mr. John Worthington, "John, this is Sarah Wiley. Could you please come to the Huxton's? The boys are fighting again."

As Gordon and Seth entered the drive, Mrs. Huxton came out screaming, "Help! Help! They have been fighting all morning." About that time Zane came running out of the house with a ball bat. "Where did he go?" he screamed. Wade ran around the outside of the barn. Zane took off after him. Wade hid a while in the barn, and silence seemed to prevail. "What happened, Mrs. Huxton?" Seth inquired. Mrs. Huxton sniffled and sobbed, "I don't know why they can't get along. I'm afraid one of them is going to get hurt. Wade stole Zane's basketball and wore his red shirt. He won't give them back, and Zane is insanely mad."

Mr. Worthington pulled up in his old beat-up truck. "What's going on?" he asked, looking puzzled, "Oma, are they fighting again?" "Yes, I'm afraid so," she blubbered. About that time, Wade ran in the house and up the stairs, with a basketball in his hand. He was wearing a bright red shirt and jeans. Zane came running after him still carrying a bat. Before anyone could get to them, Zane walloped Wade in the head with the ball bat. Blood went everywhere. Wade fell backwards and lay still and was not moving. The police had arrived. The paramedics were called, and arrived within ten minutes. After examining Wade, they pronounced him dead.

Zane was handcuffed and taken away. Mrs. Huxton sobbed with both her hands on her face, "Why, Why, did this have to happen? What am I going to do? Mr. Worthington put his hand on Oma's shoulder, "I'm so sorry, sis, I'm so sorry. Sometimes God works in mysterious ways. We will never know the purpose of these actions."

A couple months later, Zane was institutionalized. He was unstable for a trial, and the judge ordered him into the mental home.

XXVI. Highfield Academy

Sarah and her sisters felt so fortunate for their higher education, as lots of the children in the area were not so lucky. She remembered her mother insisting on a higher education for her girls. Hannah looked at Lyle and blurted out, "We want an education for our girls." Reconstruction on an old grade school in Highfield, Il., just north of Aunt Faye's, has been completed. I guess President Lincoln had made many stops through the town of Highfield and this one room school, which is now a high school. This school sounds so exciting, as there are many advantages for our children. Scholastic events, athletic challenges, and much more are offered. There are many different classrooms, and several teachers."

I am going to write a letter, and we will see if the girls can stay with Aunt Faye while they are in school."

"This sounds like a good idea to me, Hannah, and if you would like, I will mail your letter when I go into town to get us some groceries, and the school will get the letter sooner," Lyle reciprocated. "The sooner the better," Hannah responded.

Quakers had moved to Illinois in 1822 from the East and the

South to a better farm land and a non-slave state. The town of Highland became their settlement. Highland became a prospering little town. Many businesses opened, also a post office, grain elevator, and grocery store. A log church was built first and later in 1884 a new brick church was constructed. Next to the church the academy was built. The Highland Academy was formed and many came to this school for a better education. This school was the best in the county.

Highfield Academy was built in 1830 and was a grade school first starting out with just forty students. The school was supported by donations. In a few years enrollment increased to one hundred and sixty students. This was the first grade school in the county. Highfield Academy was just a log cabin with planks of wood for desks and a puncheon floor. A school bell sounded the start of classes. Quill pens were used from the family geese. In 1824 the schools enrollment was fourteen students and in 1874 Highland Academy was formed with the first gym built in 1911. This was the first gym in the county. Later as the academy grew, a high school was formed. To attend high school was quite an honor, as many could not afford to go.

Several lawyers, statesmen, and professors graduated from the academy. The Quakers moved from the Carolinas and Tennessee, getting away from slavery. The teachers were dedicated. The teachers boarded in a small rooming house next to the school. Boys stayed in homes in the community. A school newspaper, the Buzz, was written and many a student helped to print the paper.

The education was emphasized with a religious attitude. Some left home in horse and buggy to get to the school on time, and many were able to walk to school, as they lived within a short distance. From 1927 to 1931 Highland had their first volleyball team. There was a wide array of curriculum such as Latin, Virgil, Cicero, Caesar, surveying, trigonometry, English, astronomy and zoology.

Many times Abe Lincoln stopped through Highland. As a lawyer, he would consult books from the library, which was added to the construction in 1896. Abe was a prominent lawyer in Illinois, and soon became the sixteenth president of the United States.

The first year the girls moved in with Aunt Faye. "Come on in, girls. I have your room ready for you, and I emptied a closet for your clothes. This room is for guests. I think you will enjoy staying here. Just let me know if there is anything you need," Aunt Faye reminded. "Thank you, Aunt Faye, for letting us board here," Nina responded. "Mom and dad are so happy we get to go to Highfield Academy.

Aunt Faye had helped the girls out so much for giving them a home. "We love going to Highfield Academy. There are so many activities. I just think of all that I would be missing if we did not have this privilege," Nina spoke. "I am so glad I have all of you for the school year. The pleasure has been mine," Aunt Faye confirmed.

After the first year, the girls had a chance to live in a dorm in the small town of Highfield. Even though Aunt Faye's was walking distance to the school, the new dorm was even shorter distance to the school. The girls made several friends.

"Christmas break, we get a Christmas break," Paula sang in a happy tone. "I am so glad we get a Christmas break," Nina spoke. "I can't wait to see mom and dad. I am so homesick," Sarah agreed. Christmas time was a little sparse for gifts, but the thought of time together was all that mattered.

Hannah had stitched the girls a shawl for the cold weather. Each was carefully stitched and neatly blocked. The shawls were a special gift and keepsake for the girls. "Mom, I love my shawl. Thank you so much. Navy will go with everything I wear," said Paula. "We love ours, too," Sarah and Nina said in unison.

Hannah suggested they play games and sing songs. "I'll fix a home cooked meal and we'll all gather together and have some fun with our games and songs. We'll have some of my walnut brownies for dessert," Hannah suggested.

Christmas evening was a special time. All gathered around the wood stove and reminisced. "Mom your meal is delicious. We were so ready for one of your home cooked meals," Paula added. "You girls being home is the best Christmas present I could have," Lyle added. "I hope the snow holds off until we get back to school," Sarah mentioned, "but you know we will have to pack our boots. The snow will be coming."

After a few Christmas carols and all conversing, the day had ended and the family went to bed. Hannah and Lyle sat alone in the living room. Hannah said a little prayer, "Dear God, Thank you for our family, the wonderful day we spent together, and bless them all. Watch over our girls in the months to come, as they journey back to their school." In your name, Amen.

The farm economy was crippled by the great depression of the 30's and the academy was forced to close. The school was rented for different occasions and other than that was just a memory. The only buildings left in Highland, besides the church, were a few houses and only memories.

A shiny granite monument is all that remains of the school. The church remained active and members continued supporting the church.

XXVII. Sarah

Sarah was a small, petite, little girl with coal black hair. She always wanted to have her own way, and usually got what she wanted. She had three sisters. She was also a daddy's girl. "Daddy, daddy, hold me," Sarah whined. Of course, Lyle bent over, picked her up, and said, "Now, now what's wrong, Sarah? Daddy's right here. What do you want, honey?" Whatever she wanted, her daddy was always there for her. She always wanted to have her own way, and usually got what she wanted. Even her sisters gave in to her, so she wouldn't fret.

Sarah was a very intelligent girl and a quick learner. In school Sarah ranked at the top of her class. She excelled in grade school. She and her sisters rode an old hack to school, and often had to walk very far to get to their destination. Many children walked to school three or four miles. Fortunately the school hack picked the girls up and brought them home. "Get your boots on and wear warm socks, girls, the weather is going to get bad," Hannah Linzee told her children, "The old hack may be cold today." The girls did as they were told. The girls were looking and finding a warm hat and gloves. Hannah had knitted all three girls a new pair of gloves and scarves to match their coats.

Flora, Sarah's oldest sister, came down with typhoid fever. She was seven. Hannah led the family in a prayer, "Dear God please save our daughter. Seeing her suffer is so hard for all of us, and please watch over her." She was seven. The fever overcame her and she succumbed to this terrible fate. Flora's death was a very hard time for the family, and took a toll on all. The family missed Flora so very much. Knowing she was in heaven and the suffering would be over was the only comfort they were able to have.

Little Sarah contacted the fever, also. Putting cloths to her head, they tried to get the fever down. "Mommy," Sarah said, "Where's my daddy? I feel better. I want my daddy."

"Don't worry, Sarah, daddy is at work, and when he gets home, he will rock you and sing to you," encouraged Hannah.

Lyle returned home early that day. He picked Sarah up. He sat in the old family rocker and rocked and sang, "Oh! Suzanna! Don't you cry for me. I came from Alabama with a banjo on my knee! Did you like daddy's song? Do you want me to sing another song for you?" Lyle questioned. "Sing another," she mumbled. "You get a line and I'll get a pole. We'll go down to the crawdad hole," he sang. She loved her daddy and with the help from the family, she began getting better that very day. Fortunately, she was able to combat the disease. The others were lucky, and did not contact the fever,

As the girls grew up, education was their main interest. "How are we going to go on to school, mom?" Sarah asked. "I am checking with your Aunt Faye to see if we can arrange for you to live with her while you go to Highfield Academy," Hannah assured.

The year was 1927. The girls had received a letter of their acceptance at Highland Academy. This was an exciting time for them. Paula was the oldest of the girls. Sarah, Nina, and Paula were just two years apart. "Get your clothes packed girls. If any mending needs to be done, let me know. We have got to get you ready for staying with Aunt Faye," Hannah urged. This was quite a privilege as many dropped out of grade school as the times were hard. The name of the high school was Highfield Academy. The high school was one of the first in the area, as the Quakers believed in education. The school was very modern and many scholastical events and many sports events. Sarah was involved in volleyball, girl's basketball, track, and drama club. Track consisted of running, shot put, throwing the discus, long jump, high jump, and running hurdles.

"I can't wait to write mom and dad a letter," Sarah ecstatically declared, "Our track team is in the final competition for the basketball team. I just can't believe we made the finals. Who would have guessed, little ole me, would be among the finalist?" Competition with other schools was a very big event. "When you write mom and dad, don't forget to tell them, I am in the finals for the hurdles, and Paula is in the finals for the shot put," Nina added. With all of the extra curricular activities, the lives of these young girls were very busy.

"Nora, are you ready for this game tonight? Sarah inquisitively asked. Tonight was the finals in their basketball tournament. "Do you realize we are in the finals, Sarah? I am so excited. I can't calm down. Remember our special play. I want to use this play several times. Remember the ball to me, back to you, to me, and then Kate will be under the basket. We can do this all night to rack up points," Nora voiced.

The Drama Club consisted of several different functions.

Sarah joined the Drama Club, and wrote in her letters, "Mom and dad I am so thrilled to be in the Drama Club, and I am going to try out for all the plays." Junior and senior play tryouts were coming up. Sarah was so excited about the tryouts and was able to land the lead role in her senior play. The main character was Judy in "Judy, the Little Clodhopper". When she tried out for the role, no one expected for little Sarah to get the leading role. There was a little rivalry, but none had the aptitude that Sarah had. Music was not her greatest trait, but she made it through the song, "Polly Wolly Doodle". She sang a little off key, but nobody even noticed.

For their last two years, they all lived in a dorm close to the school. This was a good place to live, and they had lots of fun, sometimes getting oranges and fruit from the kitchen on off limit times and hiding them in their clothes. "Sarah, if we keep getting the fruit from the kitchen, the help is going to get suspicious of what we are doing," Nora stated. "Look, Nora, we didn't take that many, and we are hungry. Anyway oranges are healthy," Sarah calmed.

"Sarah, would you like to make some extra money to help with your schooling and school clothes?" her sister Paula questioned. I have a friend that works as a maid in the upper class area in the town nearby, Daperville, and she is leaving. She wanted to know if I knew anybody interested, and I thought of you." Sarah thought a while and then she replied, "I would be excited to help mom and dad with our school expenses and my own spending money. Tell her I am interested. A new job to earn some extra money sounds challenging to me."

In the next few months of summer time, Sarah went to work. As she entered the home, Mrs. Birkeley, her new employer, offered her a chair, "Sit down here, darling. I am glad to have you for the summer. I hope you like working here."

"I am excited about working here, and I want to thank you for the chance to do so," Sarah commented. Sarah loved her new job, and was able to room there also. She was able to save for her schooling and also buy a few clothes and other items.

The house was huge and Sarah felt like this house was a mansion. The interior was very beautiful, and the job was easy. She wrote in her letters home, "Mom, all I have to do is dust and sweep. I also do small bits of ironing which includes my own. Everything is so fancy here. The chef does the cooking and the dishes. This is a beautiful house." She was able to save each week. Her savings helped her through school.

Sarah was so homesick, she wanted to go home. She was able to go home the last three weeks of the summer. "Mom, I am glad to be home. I have missed your home cooking, and I have missed family. I have made lots of friends, but there is no place like home," Sarah admitted. "Honey, I know exactly what you mean. When I was younger and spent some time with my Aunt, I got so homesick. It was just a terrible feeling, but it is a good experience to help you grow up and realize what all you have," her mother responded.

Nina, had a few dates with Seth Wiley. He was a handsome, blue eyed, muscular young man. His eyes were stunning, being such a pretty shade of blue. Seth became interested in dating Sarah. Sarah told Nina she would not go. "Nina, you were dating Seth and I feel like I should not go," "Nina said, "This does not matter, and you will go." Nina chased her around the table, and said, "You will go!"

Saturday night a group from church and friends would get together. Seth invited Sarah to go with him. She gave in and accepted a date with him, but she reluctantly went and told Nina she was thinking she should not go.

"Okay, fellows! role the rug back. Let's get this party

started. I brought my French harp," Seth proudly broadcast. "Grab your partner, swing her to the left and swing her to the right. Everybody start dancing," Seth began leading the square dance with these verses, "Dosey do and promenade, grab her, kiss her, and swing her around, and we'll all end up down town." Seth laughed as he made up a few words as he went. He put the French harp in his pocket and grabbed Sarah. "Come on, Sarah, we're going to dance," he said as he motioned for Kate to play the piano. He was really good with the French harp and dancing was so much fun. Sarah had a wonderful evening, and starting dating Seth again. The first date had been so special.

XXVIII. Seth

Seth grew up in the country. He was the second oldest of six children. Seth's oldest brother, Harmon, was studying to become a minister. Harmon was a wonderful person, and being a minister was a natural profession for him. He assisted the neighbor, Rebecca Alt, in caring for their daughter, Effie, who had taken ill with polio. Staying at her bedside, he began a prayer. "Dear, God, please help Effie to get better, and to fight this disease. As I watch her suffer, please help her to cope with this terrible disease."

Harmon contacted the disease himself, and died at an early age of nineteen. When Harmon became ill, Seth had to drop out of school. "Seth, I am so sorry you have to drop out of school," Harmon input. "Don't worry, Harmon, I will be okay. Just try to get better. That is all I care about. I want you to get better." Seth was a sophomore, and this was his last year was able to attend school. He worked hard and helped his parents with the farming and the family.

"Hurry, Tiera, we're going to be late for school. Blake, you and Gabriel grab your books. We have to start walking or we will be late," Seth ordered. Walking to and from school each Monday through Friday was a normal occurrence unless the weather was bad. One half hour and you could be there. A small country store was located adjacent from the red brick school house, which later became known as Daisey's. Seth helped his mom and dad with all the farm work and caring for his younger sister and brothers.

Seth's one and only sister, Tiera, was a pretty young lady with auburn hair like her mother. She was very eloquent and fluent. She was a talented pianist, and spent much of her time practicing classical music. She later in years married an older man, Matt Rous, and moved away.

Seth's brother, Blake, was the black sheep of the family. He ventured away from home as soon as he turned seventeen. He began having a drinking problem. He led a rough life, lots of women and a wild life. His mother grieving over his disappearance upset her terribly. She turned ill with sinus infection. She went to the hospital, after some surgery, the infection spread throughout her body. She did not recover, and passed away at the early age of fifty-one.

Blake pawned some of his own mother's jewelry for his life style of spending. He later settled down, and married. He became a chef in a very large and fancy restaurant. He never returned home not even for his parent's funerals or his brothers. The friction between the family was too great for him to return.

Abram and Gabriel were the youngest boys. They were only eight and nine when their mother passed away. They had to fend for themselves and missed their mother very much, and life was not so easy for them after that. Of course, Seth and Tiera were there for them.

When the war came the younger boys had to go to war and

the oldest boy, which was Seth had to stay home and help with the farm. Abram joined the Navy, and Gabriel was a soldier in the army.

"Dad, we have a lot of plowing left in the back acreage. I will get on that later, but I am going to have to work on the plow first. I think I can fix the lever. The lever just seems to not be engaging the plow deep enough into the soil. I've had that problem before. I can have this fixed within the hour. I just need to grease the the bolts and gears," Seth stated as he motioned for his dad to look at the plow. "Son, why don't you let me help you? I can work on the chicken coup later. I'm getting ready for the new baby chicks. Sarah and Grace are going to have one hundred baby chicks coming next week, but I have plenty of time. Setting the brooder house up won't take long," Noah added, "Oh, I don't want to forget we need to mend the fence before the cows get out. I have some new fence we can add. This job is a must, or we will be sorry."

Seth was the leader of the family now. He helped his father farm and helped with the younger children. Seth and his brothers went to pick blackberries for homemade pies. "Look over there, Gabriel and Abram, there is a whole bunch of blackberries. Start picking," Seth ordered, "Don't sit down, as the chiggers will you eat you up and you will itch for days. Those chiggers will drive you nuts."

"Oh, shucks, I already sat down," Abram screamed, "I hope I don't start itching."

Seth loved life, and was a hard worker, happy, and contented. His smile was one of his most prominent features. He had an easy going attitude, and took a lot to provoke him. The one thing Marly learned from her father was his pleasant spirit and ability to get along with anybody. He was a great inspiration for all who knew him.

"Abram and Gabriel, are you going to watch me box tonight?" coached Seth.

"We have a tournament at the legion hall at two o'clock this afternoon. If you want to go, you can ride with me. I'm boxing the winner of last weeks match, Todd Faust. He was so good. I really have a match waiting for me."

"Sure, Seth, we're your greatest fans. Didn't you know that?" Abram acclaimed.

Seth had self-help remedies for illnesses. For stomach ache he recommended the bark of the slippery elm. Heading out to the woods, he motioned, "Here try some, Abram. You just skin the bark off, and chew on the rest, and this is great for stomach ache."

"I don't think I want any," Abram squinted and shrugged. "Maybe when we're here we'll find some paw paws. Have you had any? They taste like bananas," he exclaimed, "They are sooo good!"

Marrying Sarah, he was so proud. He thought she was so beautiful. She had coal black hair, and so trim. When she married, she weighed 98 pounds. He helped her choose her dresses. Sarah would don a hat looking as though she were on the first page of a magazine. On a shopping spree, Nina, her sister, said, "Look, Sarah, this hat matches your outfit." She had on a burgundy color dress, and the hat was black with a small burgundy feather. "I think you are right, Nina; I'll just buy this hat and put it on now," Sarah proudly assented. Away they went walking down the sidewalk. Of course, this was November and a cold windy day. A brisk wind just picked her hat up and started blowing the hat down the street. Nina and Sarah are chasing and trying to catch the hat. "Oh, it's under a car," shouted Nina. "Oh, no, I hope it's not dirty," cried Sarah, as she poked a stick under the car to retrieve the hat. Luckily, the new hat was in one piece and away they went home. Seth was waiting in the car a block away by the court house. They were telling him of the incident, and all started laughing. Seth laughed and said, "I wish I could have seen you two running after the hat!"

Right after they were married, both had just fallen asleep. A loud noise woke them up. "What was that noise?" Sarah whispered. "I don't know. I'll check it out," Seth whispered back. A bunch of their friends were at the door with a wheel barrow. Pans were clattering, whistles and horns were in the background. "Get up, we're going on a ride down the road," Abram shouted. "Oh, no, Seth, I am so embarrassed. I have on my gown. What will I do?" Sarah cried. "I don't know, just follow me, everything will be okay," Seth assured. In these days chivalry was very popular. The custom was to surprise the married couple. They both were put into the wheel barrow in their pajamas and everyone following and laughing. This was a night they would not forget!

XXIX. Down in the Country

Seth gestured for the girls and Sarah to set on the wagon by the huge water tank. "Sarah, you and the girls want to ride with me to water the hogs? Sit up on the wagon. Hang on," he motioned, "We may hit a few craters in the road. We're going to water the hogs and you all can ride along." This was so much fun to ride on the big wagon and watch the hogs come near. They were waiting for their water.

"Going back to the house, how about you driving the tractor, Jeanie?" Seth urged. This one particular time, rounding the curve, the wheel turned on the tractor, but Jeanie made a wise move, and let the wheel twist, and after the incident was over, Seth in a complimentary voice stated, "Good job, sis, you handled that well."

"Thanks, dad, I was scared, but I held on," Jeanie replied.

Their driving skills came from driving the ole 52 Chevy back into the acreage. With a stick shift, learning to drive was a lot of hops and jumps. "Slow, down," Marly screamed, "You're going too fast." They would laugh and hop, laugh and hop.

Marly started telling her knock knock jokes which she thought was hilarious. Of course, Jeanie was getting a little tired of them. “Jeanie, I got a joke for you. Do you know what you wash the telephone with?” Marly questioned. “I don’t know, what? “ Jeanie replied. “Dial soap,” Marly answered with a chuckle. “I have another one for you. Knock knock,” Marly asked. “Who’s there?” Jeanie added. “Candy,” Marly said. “Candy who?” Jeanie added. “Can’t he come out tonight. Ha Haa,” Marly laughed and laughed. I have just one more. I promise. “Knock knock,” Marly asked again. “Who’s there now?” Jeanie responded. “Police,” Marly stated. “Okay, police who?” Jeanie asked. “Please pass the sugar, ha ha ha,” Marly laughed. “Marly, you’re nuttier than a fruitcake,” Jeanie joked. “One more Jeanie and I will quit. Have you heard the joke about the rope?” Marly voiced. “No,” replied Jeanie. “Oh, skip it,” Marly remarked, “Ha, Ha, ha, that was a good one!”

For anyone learning to drive a stick shift, getting the hang of smooth driving takes a while. “Jeanie, slow down!” screamed Marly. “Oh, nuts, I’m doing okay, and I think it’s fun to go faster,” said Jeanie. Good thing there were plenty of open fields. “Mom, Jeanie drove so fast, I was scared pea green! Tell her next time to slow down!” Marly begged. “Oh my goodness, now Jeanie, don’t you ever drive fast again, or we’ll have to quit letting you and Marly drive in the back fields,” Sarah reprimanded.

Seth and Sarah planted a large garden every year. They referred this garden as the truck patch. The truck patch provided enough vegetables for canning. “You girls can weed the gardens. When you weed the cucumbers, don’t step on the vines or they will die. Take the hoe and hand cultivator and get started. Take a jug of water with you. You’re going to need it,” Seth ordered. “I get the cultivator. I love using the cultivator. I hate pulling the weeds," Marly groaned. "Let's just get it done," Jeanie stated, "Just think about having the garden tilled, and we can come back to the house and relax."

Both girls ventured down to the truck patch. "I'll start with this row of tomatoes," Marly said. "Ohh! I can't stand it. Here's a green worm. Ewww! Look at it, Jeanie!" Over came Jeanie and shouted, "It's just a tomato worm. Keep weeding." Planting a small garden close to the house was very convenient also. Fresh vegetables were a great addition to the home cooked meals. A grape arbor was nearby, and Sarah made the best grape juice and grape jelly.

After fussing to go fishing, the family all got their gear ready and set out to go fishing. As they were walking, Norman's fishing pole stuck Jeanie in the eye. The next day her eye swelled up real big. Seth got out a steak, and he put this steak on her eye. The old-fashioned belief was this would draw out the infection. The doctor said, "You might as well have eaten that steak, because that is an old wive's tale and there is no truth in it at all."

In 1955, Elvis and the Beatles' songs were all the rage. "Tonight on Channel 3 we are going to watch films of Elvis in Europe and his trip home. I can't wait," Norman joyously announced. All gathered around the t.v. that evening, watching Elvis and relaxing in their pajamas.

Norman purchased a new transistor radio. A record player was every girl's wish. The girl's cousins gave them a new 45 r.p.m. record player. Play a record, and then put the next one on.

"The plumbers will have the pipes installed for running water on Friday. Aren't you excited about that, Sarah? Mr. Veneer told me he would install a new bathroom next," Seth elated. "Just think, Seth, running water. No more carrying water. This will take some getting use to. I have dreamed of this day!" exhilarated Sarah.

Inside plumbing was the best thing that ever happened, but Seth had some time adjusting. He still ventured out to the old outhouse with his magazine. Marly could never understand that.

XXX. Surgery

Dental work was definitely going to be a part of Marly's life. Marly looked in the mirror and cried many times. "Mom, what am I going to do?" she coaxed her mom, "Can we go to the dentist soon?" "I was hoping with time your teeth would straighten and fall in place, but I know this is a problem. I called the dentist this morning, and we have an appointment in July to see what can be done," she informed Marly. Marly thought to herself, "I hope something can be done. I know fixing my teeth can change my life." Marly had many friends, but her self-esteem was very low. Being so self-conscious of her teeth was dragging her down. She couldn't wait to see the local dentist, Mr. Kirst.

The appointment was at 9:00 a.m. They arrived on time and sat down in the comfy waiting room. Doctor Kirst came out of the office into the waiting room and spoke with Seth and Sarah, "I have taken x-rays of Marly's teeth and the only solution I can see is to pull the front two teeth and a bridge fitted into her mouth. Of course, we will have to do a little surgery which can be done in the office."

August first of 1960, she went into surgery. The doctor began the surgery, which was performed in the office. The protruding bone was chiseled down, and two teeth were to be bridged in between the good teeth after the healing. After the surgery, she was sent home to recuperate. She lay in bed feeling miserable, but so glad the operation was over. “Mom, my mouth feels so big and full. The medicine is starting to wear off. Can I have another pill?” Marly asked. “You have to wait one more hour and I can give you a couple of aspirin. Tomorrow will be much easier. The swelling will go down,” Sarah consoled.

“Mom, somebody is at the door,” Jeanie yelled from the bedroom. “Come in, Diana,” Sarah motioned. “I heard about Marly’s surgery, and I brought her a card,” Diana expressed. “Jeanie and Marly are in the bedroom. Marly has to keep comfortable and not move around. The surgery took a lot out of her. She will be okay, just a trying day. Jeanie is helping make sure she is comfortable,” Sarah spoke. As Diana walked in, she gave Marly a card, “Here, Marly, let me see your mouth. Ohh! Does that hurt! I feel for you. I brought you a couple of magazines and one crossword puzzle book.”

“Thanks,” Marly mumbled. “My family sends their best wishes,” Diana assured.

Being home in the summer time from school was helpful, as she spent most of her time at home. “Marly, Cara called and wants you to come to town tonight and spend the night with her. What do you think?” Sarah asked. “No, I don’t want to go. I’ll just stay home,” Marly reacted. The healing and adjustment took most of her summer.

Getting back to school was great. Marly was very elated. She felt like a new person. Marly had so many friends, and was so glad to be back.

"Mom, I got in trouble at school today. You would never believe what happened," Marly addressed to her mother. "I was so bored in the study hall, I decided to paint my nails. Jeff next to me asked me to paint his thumb nail. I started painting different thumb nails of the boys sitting around me in the study hall. Mr. Miller, our social studies teacher, was in charge of the huge study hall. He heard the commotion I was making. He said, "Marly, come and sit up front for the rest of the study hall." I was so embarrassed. I learned my lesson. You know what else happened, mom? Mary told Mr. Miller in our social studies class, he was her favorite teacher. Guess what he said? You will not believe," Marly rambled. "Well, I don't know, what did he say?" Sarah asked. "He said, "Well, pick my nose."

"I am so appalled a teacher would make that comment," she stated.

"You know what else, Mom? Two boys in the class were making fun of one of our teachers. Her false teeth slipped out once," Marly rambled on. "Look, Marly, my mom always taught me if you can't say something good about someone, don't say anything at all."

For an assignment in literature, Marly wrote the following essay:

THE STUDY HALL IS FOR STUDYING

The study hall is for studying. I was sitting in the first study hall with nothing to do, so I thought. As I was gazing around, the boy next to me, saw I was starting to paint my nails. His name was Jeff. Jeff said, "Will you paint my thumb nail?" Of course, I was glad to do that. The next thing I had painted all the thumb nails of the guys around me. I thought this would be rather humorous to see a bunch of boys with nail polish on their thumb nails. By this time I guess I was attracting a lot of attention. Well, I was painting all the boys' thumb nails around me. None of the kids objected to the polish; so, I guess, I had plenty to do now.

About the last one to paint, I not only had the pupil's attention, I also had the teacher's. The teacher, Mr. Miller, beckoned to me. I walked up to the desk. Was it embarrassing! He shouted, "Sittttt!" I said, "May I please get my book?" His reply again was sit!!! So I went over to the seat he was pointing at and sat. I opened a book out of the desk. Do you think I read? I was too embarrassed. Everybody was staring, but I thought the bell would ring eventually. Well, the bell never rang, seeming like five hours even though just thirty minutes. I thought after the bell rang, this event would be over. I was fooled. My friends I met as I was walking to class said, "Hey, Marly, why did you move up by the teacher's desk?" I exclaimed, "Well, it's a long story, but I did learn one thing, the study hall is for studying."

After the dental surgery, Marly's life changed.Shopping for new clothes, new hair style, and her popularity increased. Her junior year she was nominated homecoming queen. Sarah was very excited for her. They went shopping for a formal, and beads, and heels. "Look, Marly, how about this one," replied Sarah. The formal was pink which they accented with pink beads and earrings to match. After a long day of shopping, all went home. "Man, my feet are tired," Jeanie complained. "I'll fix us some grill cheese and tomato soup. You girls just relax. This won't take long," Sarah replied.

The night of the homecoming had arrived. She walked out onto the gym floor with the other contestants at half time of the basketball game. Wearing heels was a challenge, and as she went she bit her lip, and not realizing it. Walking in heels was a new experience for her. She practiced at home walking and walking, posing and posing, trying to look at ease. Being nominated for homecoming queen was quite an honor and a great experience. Diana, the senior nominee, won the competiton. Most often, the senior nominee was the winner.

XXXI. A New Job

Just finishing her junior year, Marly looked forward to the summer. A manager of a local truck stop came by to see if Marly would work for him. "Come on in," Sarah remarked as she opened the door. "Hello, I am Mr. Bale and I am the manager and owner of the diner, The Country Inn Diner on Fourth Street. I was wondering if Marly would like to come and work for me?" Mr. Bale spoke. "Mr. Bale, Marly does not have any experience. I am not sure this job is for her."

"Even though she has no experience, I will train her," Mr. Bale replied. "I guess I can give this job a try, but because I do not have any experience, and I feel like this is not for me," Marly addressed.

Her first day on the job was quite an experience. The customers seem to drawl their order out. "I want the special of the day, ham and beans with cornbread. I like plenty of corn bread," the customer ranted. Being a little incoherent, he could not pronounce his order clearly. He definitely had been drinking. Marly couldn't understand him at all.

"Mr. Bale, can you help me with this order," Marly asked. He came to her rescue and finished with the customer's order.

She finally improved with taking the orders, but hated the job, and liked meeting the people. Waitress work was not for her.

She was very naive and gullible. Always believing everyone was truthful as she was, made a difficult time adjusting. Seth and Sarah were starting to have some free time. They were able to dine out, and enjoying their moments together, as always. They dined at the new restaurant, but Marly was not working the day they went.

"Seth, I am going to make you a doctor's appointment. I know you are not feeling well, and Dr. Zorrick is open late two nights of the week. How about Thursday night?" Sarah demanded. "I know you're right, Sarah, but I have lots of work to catch up on. I have to plow the acreage behind the house before the weather turns bad. Mr. Veneer wants me to paint the shed and mend some fence. I guess something might have to wait," Seth unwillingly agreed.

Seth had such determination and hardworking spirit. Seth just didn't want to give up and admit that he was not feeling well. He felt indispensable. "Sarah, how will my work get done, if I leave," he asked.

"Sarah made the appointment on a Thursday. As they entered the office, Dr. Zorrick welcomed him into the patient room. He examined Seth and announced, "Well, Seth, you have more than one thing. If you want we will just do more than one surgery, and get the whole thing done. You have a fissure, which is a crack in the bowel which will require minor surgery, but necessary. You also have a hernia. You know I am thinking you may have a ruptured appendix. I want you to enter the hospital today."

"I knew something was wrong, just didn't want to admit it," Seth responded. Seth, Sarah, and the girls headed to the hospital. Luckily Sarah thought ahead, and packed a suitcase for Seth.

Seth did have a ruptured appendix, a fissure, and a hernia. He had the operations, and was a mighty sick man. He would be fine after a few weeks. He needed just a little recuperation time. Sarah and family visited which helped through the transformation. Visiting him three or four times a week and bringing him magazines and snacks made the time go fast.

Coming home from the hospital, Sarah looked at Marly and questioned, "Marly will you get the coal bucket and bring some coal in? The fires are getting low. We can't let them go out. Lord, I think they already have. Sure seems cold in here."

"Mom, I can't wait till dad gets out of the hospital. It has been three weeks, and I miss him. I know he is homesick, too," Marly confirmed. Seth was homesick and he finally got to leave the hospital. Three weeks was a long time to be away.

"I have saved enough money from my job to get me a new stereo. When we go see dad, I would like to pick the stereo up. I can't wait to get it," Marly excitedly explained. "Where did you see this stereo?" Sarah questioned. "I was shopping, and I went in the new furniture store in Calesburg. There it was. I love it and I can't wait till you see it," explained Marly. On the next trip to the hospital, the stereo was purchased. Marly had enough money for one record, a Johnny Mathis record. Everyday she listened to the new stereo and radio.

Sarah offered to let Marly paint her room lavender. "Try not to spill the paint or get the paint on the woodwork," coached Sarah. When she was done painting, Sarah spoke, "For Pete sakes, Marly, you have paint from head to toe. You are going to have to take a bath." She had paint everywhere. Sarah cleaned and cleaned to get the mess up. Sarah made some lavender doilies to match. The room turned out beautiful.

"Mom, my friend, Sonya at school is going steady with Evan. She and a lot of the other girls wrap angora around their boyfriend's rings, so they would fit. It really looks weird. Sonya even used tape and finger nail polish. What do you think about that?" Marly questioned. "Good night, what are they going to do next? Sarah reacted.

On top of Marly's dresser, she had several bottles of nail polish, a color for every outfit. Marly was very feminine and always tried to look her best.

"Jeanie and Marly, if you would, while I am recuperating would you clean out the two hog houses out at the hog lot by the gate. Stay away from the sows, as they can be pretty mean. The sows are so protective of their little ones, they won't allow anyone near them," Seth ordered. "Okay, dad, we will do that tomorrow," Jeanie assured. The girls headed to the barn, stopping at the pole shed to get the shovels. "Jeanie, I don't think I want to marry a farmer," Marly laughed. "I know I am not," said Jeanie. This was the last time either of them cleaned a hog house.

"Mom, a bulletin came across the t.v.," Marly mentioned. "This was such a bleak moment. Do you know what this is all about?" "What did the bulletin say?" Sarah responded. "In large letters the bulletin read "Cuban Crisis. This really scares me. We need to listen to the news tonight."

Things were back to normal. School functions and neighbor outings kept all of the family busy. "Dad I have a basketball game tonight. I hope you and mom can make it to the game. Tonight is a home game, and should be a good game. Norman was the star player. Watching him play that night, Seth yells, "Get the ball, Norm. Pass the ball to Norm." Sarah wrenched her hands in her handkerchief, and yelled, "Go, Norm, go." Watching Norman was so exciting. Norman was top scorer with thirty-nine points. The game went into overtime with Norman making the final winning foul shot. What a night!

The following week was awards night. Mr. Planty, the principal, introduced the basketball players. “Tonight we are starting out with our most prestigious award, the VIP award. This award goes to Norman Wiley. He is a team player. Norman has shown good sportsmanship, and he is the top scorer for the team. He is just a perfect example for a team player. Norman would you come forward and get your award?” Mr. Planty directed.

Norman in a shy manner, nodded, and spoke softly, “Thank you, Mr. Planty. I appreciate this award very much.”

XXXII. The Car Wreck

Norman had graduated, and was working in a plastic factory. Norman became ill and was in the hospital for a while. Breathing the chemical fumes, Norman had came down with severe headaches and itching. Sarah cried and cried. It was a hard time as Norman was having a rough time. Norman had loaned Marly his car, a small sport car. "Marly, you can use my car while I am in the hospital," Norman suggested. Norman was very close to Marly and always helped her out. She headed into work and on a sharp curve the car started swaying out of control. The engine being in the back of the car, and the light front end made the car sway after a speed of fifty. This should have been a warning for her, but she did not realize until too late. Marly never told anyone of the incident, and she let it slide.

Marly set out to see her girl friend, Nanine. "Mom, I'm upset about Norman being sick. I'm going to go to Nanine's house. I will be back soon," Marly insisted. "Are you sure you want to go, supper will be ready soon?" Sarah hinted. Nanine lived about two to three miles away.

After leaving Nanine's house the car got out of control on

the gravel road. She began swaying back and forth, and the car swerved and she hit a two foot cement post in a wide open field about one and one-half miles from her home. When hitting the loose gravel, she panicked. She through her hands in the air, and that was all she remembered.

The neighbors heard the noise, saw the wreck out at the end of their drive, and called the ambulance. Marly's body fell in between the seats. A farm hand, Roy Cade, came running to the car. He saw Marly laying there.

His long arms were able to pull her body from between the seats, and soon she was in the ambulance. The bone in her left leg was protruding through the skin. She had a compound fracture. She was in shock. Her head had a gash very close to the temple of her left eye. A little over she would have died instantly. She was bleeding profusely. Her leg was starting to clot which kept her from bleeding to death.

Sarah answered the phone, "Hello, this is Sarah. Is Marly all right? "There's been an accident and Marly is seriously injured. Come to the Wilson's, the house east of Nanine's. The ambulance is coming. Hurry!" Nanine's mother emotionally spoke. Upon arriving Marly was in the ambulance, speaking to her mother she said, "Hi Mom," Don't worry I'm alright." Of course, she was in shock and she did not remember speaking any words to her mother. Jeanie, Seth, and Sarah all headed to the hospital, scared of what to face and what was going to happen. Marly was in surgery several hours. Family members patiently waited, and prayed for her.

After surgery and returning to her room, she heard a voice. Her brother Gordon was yelling, "You've been in a car wreck, can you hear me?" He repeated this over and over, and gradually Marly began to hear him. She had bandages and thirteen stitches on the left side of her face. She was a very lucky young girl.

The next day bright and early in the morning, Marly went into surgery. Her parents walked down the hallway with her as the nurses pushed the hospital bed. She was transported to the operating room. "Don't worry, Marly, the operation will soon be over, and you will be back in the room," her daddy assured. "We'll see you then. Here, let mom kiss your head," her mother whispered in her ear.

Marly's pelvis was fractured. She came out of surgery with a contraption on her right foot. All the toes and arch was broken in her right foot. Her toes were strung with wires the shape of a frog foot. Doctor Kibbens spoke with the family, "I want you to know the right foot may be in too much pain to leave like this, but we will try it." Her hip and leg were put in traction. A rod was run through her left heel. A triangle was placed at the top of the bed to pull herself up. When the bed moved, she could feel the bones in her left leg jiggle.

One of the nurses peaked around the door and said, "Honey, nurse Jane will be in to change your sheets within the hour."

"Oh no,"Marly thought, "This is going to hurt." As nurse Jane entered with the other nurse, Mia, she spoke softly, "Now we have to change the sheets. If we don't you can get bed sores, and we don't want that." As they lifted her up, Marly groaned with pain, but the new fresh sheets felt so good, and the pain subsided.

Marly had some bad burns on her knees from radio wires. "Now, look, Marly do not pick at these burns as they will scab over. The burns are healing. I want them to heal. If you keep picking at them, you will get infection," Sarah reprimanded.

The pain in her right foot was crucial. Dr. Kibbens was right; the pain was unbearable. She woke up in the middle of the night begging for a pain killer. "Nurse, nurse, help me! It hurts," Marly sobbed and sobbed. Eventually her sobbing became uncontrollable. The nurses came running, "Honey, don't worry you will be all right, just be patient. You will get better," the nurses urged. Morphine was given her every four hours. This was the only relief she could get. After the morphine, she felt as if she was on the ocean. She could hear the waves moving and bouncing. "Is it time yet? Can I have more morphine? Marly begged.

She kept reminding herself that she was the one to blame and no one else. She would have to be strong and this would make her stronger. Marly reminded herself different trials and tribulations in life make you stronger. Lots of flowers were sent. Friends and family came to visit. "Oh, I'm so glad your pretty face is not ruined," one of her friends from the restaurant exclaimed. Lots of cards were sent to her home and the hospital and thirteen flower arrangements lined her room. A stuffed animal from her classmate hung from the top of her bed.

The doctor was driving past the Wiley residence. He said to himself, "I have just got to go tell them." He drove up the long lane, and Sarah answered the door, "Come on in, doctor. Is Marly all right?" she asked. The doctor slowly answered, "Well, Sarah, there is something I must tell you. The small red dots on her skin are a sign of infection. If the infection does not subside, I am afraid we will have to amputate. I am sorry I have to tell you this, but I have to let you know." Sarah started sobbing, as Seth entered the room. The doctor continued to explain to Seth, but Seth was optimistic, and he said, "Look, doctor, she is a mighty spunky girl, and I think she will be all right."

With the concussion, Marly's vision had doubled. The picture vision was perfect, but there were two of everything. The doctors assured her that this would leave, and leave it did.

Her mother and dad came to visit every day. Sarah brought pretty little pajamas and gowns. "Look what I bought today, red and white pj's with hearts. I also bought some dry shampoo, and maybe this will make your hair fresher," Sarah encouraged Marly.

Uncle Mose wife, Dora, came to visit with a present, also. She did not really know Marly that well, but she was very sympathetic and wanted to help and encourage Marly all she could. Classmates brought presents and came to visit. She learned to crochet and embroider for hobbies.

After coming home from the hospital, Sarah kept her busy, and helped fix meals that were nourishing. Ten weeks had been a long time. She had gained some weight due to the sundaes and milk shakes everyone brought her. "Okay, Marly, I am going to count calories in the foods I give you and we will be able to take off the excess weight you have gained," Sarah commented, "With lack of exercise no wonder you started gaining the weight. Good gracious! All those sundaes and milk shakes everybody brought you."

"It will be hard, mom, but with your help maybe I can do it," murmured Marly. She gradually started losing, and began looking great.

Marly was able to study at home and finished her first semester at home. This was her senior year. After ten weeks in the hospital, she was dismissed with casts on both legs. Dr. Messick, her bone doctor, came to check on her one last time before she left. She was able to be dismissed. "Here," he said, "I'll lift you into the wheel chair," enjoying every moment. She just didn't understand the doctor. He was trying to make her feel comfortable, but comfortable she was not. October was here and the leaves were beautiful, beautiful colors of orange, green and browns.

Being disabled to walk was an adjustment. An elderly friend and neighbor came to visit quite often. She smoked and yakked constantly. Sarah would get a little impatient with her. Sarah was looking out the window to see if her husband was picking her up yet, and she caught her doing it. "Look, Sarah, he will be here soon to pick me up, and I hope I haven't overstayed my welcome, and remember a watchpot never boils," the neighbor insisted. She had definitely overstayed her welcome and was starting to get annoying.

"We'll work a jigsaw puzzle tonight, Marly. We'll just leave the puzzle on the dining room table until we are finished," Sarah encouraged. Sarah helped Marly all through her recuperation, keeping her busy.

Jeanie stayed with Marly on a fall afternoon while Seth and Sarah went with Lee and his family to fall harvest festival. She announced, "Marly, I am going to get married. I have met a man that I am in love with. I have not known him long, but I have made my decision."

"Are you sure you want to get married?" Marly quizzed. Marly thought in her own mind, "This decision has to be hers, and I must not interfere."

Being in a wheel chair was depressing. The doctors removed the right cast, but before they removed the cast, Dr. Kibben was very honest and said. "Marly you and your parents must realize the right foot will have a bump on the vamp of your foot. This is the best we could do. Your foot was totally crushed."

"I understand, and I am so thankful for the fact that you saved my foot, that I can handle a small bump," Marly complimented. Gradually Marly graduated to a walker and then crutches. Fighting depression was the hardest. "Marly we will get you some hobbies and reading material," Seth remarked, "You will keep busy and this will help."

Sarah kept busy being a caretaker for Marly. Marly began flourishing with her help. In the meantime Sarah kept busy with her crafts. "Marly, I have a craft book that shows how to make a rug with old outgrown winter coats. I am going to make this rug. Each coat remnant will bring us memories," she excitedly announced. "Can you use my coat I loved so much? This coat is too little for me now?" The coat was green and yellow. I also had a red coat," Marly remarked with delight. "I have several family outgrown coats of all colors. First I have to cut the wool into strips, and I then buy some strong cotton material for the backing, and sew these strips onto the material. I then slash these strips in one fourth inch sections. This should be very pretty, and this will be a keepsake," Sarah commented.

XXXII. Graduation

Marly's goal was to walk to her graduation. Getting close to the last doctor's appointment, Sarah spoke to Seth, "I hope this is the time to remove the cast. Seems like each appointment had been discouragement for Marly. He is always stating another month."

"Sarah, you know taking xrays will enable the doctors know when the leg is ready for the cast to be removed. Be patient," Seth assured. The next appointment Marly's daddy carried her to the car. He loaded her up, and away they went. The doctor removed the cast and an x'ray was taken. As the doctor came out, he spoke with sincerity, "Marly, I am sorry, but we have to recast and another three months is needed."

Her daddy carried her junior queen candidate picture on him. "You want to see a picture of my daughter?" Seth asked the woman sitting in the waiting room. He then explained what happened. "Oh, she is beautiful," the lady responded. She then went on to explain why she was sitting in the room, "My husband lost his arm in a farming accident. The combine was running, and he pulled a corn stock out and his arm was sucked right in. He is getting along fine. He'll be in to see Marly tomorrow. He is sedated now and sleeping." Seth went on to explain to the lady that at the time of the wreck, the left leg had splintered a piece of bone off, and she had to wait until this bone filled in. Several trips to the doctor, and finally after eleven months, the cast was removed.

Lots of therapy followed. Determination followed. She went with a walking cast on her left leg, to school. At school walking stairs was very difficult. She managed, and classmates were very helpful for carrying her books. "This is so hard, walking with crutches up the stairs, Cary," Marly stated. "Don't worry, Marly, I'll carry your books. I'll be there to help you. Just take your time," Cary encouraged.

The right foot and ankle had mended well enough for the cast to be removed. "I am so glad to have the cast removed. The doctors had reminded her the right foot would have a small bump, because the break was hard to set. I can handle a small bump on my foot," Marly anxiously replied. She was so thankful, and at one point, the doctor did not know if her left leg was going to mend. He removed the cast on the left leg, and after the x-ray, replaced the cast and said, "We have to allow another ten weeks, and then we will see if your leg is strong enough." After two months, the doctor agreed to remove the cast.

If you are going to walk to graduation, you are going to have to put forth effort," Seth and Sarah persisted. After the casts were removed, dead skin cells had to be removed and her skin was oiled. Because of her immobility, the joints had become painful. Her joints swelled from having the casts on so long. Each day was gradual improvement.

"You can do it, Marly," her mother suggested. "Start walking between these two trees out in the front yard," she urged, "Back and forth once, and each day keep adding a little more distance." Marly walked back and forth with a slight limp, but she kept up and each day a little more, never giving up.

The class went on a senior trip to Chicago. Her classmates wanted her to go, but she knew in her heart she was not ready for walking long distances. She went, but walking was very difficult for her. Marly's ankle began swelling. The foot was very sore. "Mom I am so glad to be home. Walking so far really hurt. I knew I shouldn't have gone. My foot and ankle hurt so bad," she commented.

Marly was able to walk to her graduation. She graduated magna cum laude. She was valedictorian and delivered a graduation farewell speech. She welcomed everyone (faculty, board members, parents and students). Marly began her speech with great pride and confidence and began blurting the written speech out,

"As we bid farewell to you tonight, we realize our graduation exercises would be incomplete without your presence, and our parting from the school would be sad without your good wishes.

How great it is to be here. My classmates and I are looking forward to a bright future. We feel we can become what we want to be and conquer any obstacles along the way. In this distant future we will be hard workers and be dedicated to our goals. My thanks go to the administration and faculty for teaching us how to maintain our goals.

We have worked hard to arrive at our destination. Twelve years of school has brought us to this place in our lives. We can now go on and further our careers, for whatever choices we have made.

It has been said that opportunity knocks but once at every man's door. Our future rests with him. Let us hope we recognize him, for whose coming we so trustingly wait, and upon who so much depends.

I have always followed a positive thinking attitude. I believe in keeping a good attitude and outlook. This helps to mold you to become what you are to become. Set your goals high and you will succeed. Your attitude is number one. Be a friend, and you will have many. Remember sunshine in your face is sunshine to the world. Sunshine in your smile will put sunshine in the air. Each day I make my day the fullest and most rewarding, and my classmates and I will walk from this school with great destinations and goals in mind.

We are going to work hard to accomplish what we strive to be. We hope we achieve all the above and to be successful at our chosen career. We are forever thankful to you. We hope from what we have learned from this school, Kingsley High, that we can move forward and become what we want to be. We will never give up and make the most of what we have. We are very excited to move forward with our new careers and choices. We hope to make you proud."

As we leave here, we leave with a smile on our face and lots of good memories. Farewell to you all and thanks for everything.

I thank you.

She was not nervous, but just thankful she was able to deliver her speech and walk to her graduation. Her leg was still hurting from the swelling and would probably never be the same. She had overcome this obstacle and was heading on for new destinations, just as her speech stated.

XXXIV. Time Passed By Fast

Lots of years had passed by, children, happy times, heartaches, parties, and celebrations. Lee was retired and a grandpa living in the country. He began reminiscing about his childhood, and he decided to walk back to the old tree he carved his name on. He called his friends. "Hey, Chuck, how about you and Barry going with me on a hike to the old beech tree I carved my name on several years ago. Let's see if the tree is still standing."

"Sure, Lee, I'll call Barry and we will head over in my jeep," Chuck replied. "Boy, these woods will bring back lots of memories for us."

" Do you think there are any logs left from the fort we built back here by the crick? Remember when Gordon worked for weeks on the roof, and when it rained the sides and top were too weak and caved in. Finally he got some stronger wood, and he rebuilt the fort," Lee rambled on. "That fort was so strong, I bet it is still standing. If it weren't so far out in the woods, we would go check it out. I'm not sure I could walk that far now."

After getting permission, he and his two long time friends

drove the truck down the lane past the barn, (the same old, weathered barn where they had many a corncob fight), parked the truck, got out, and started walking back through the woods to the tree he carved his name on.

There it was! All the large trees had been cut down except the one he carved his name on. Just as plain as day, the ole beech tree, bigger than ever, carved in the tree, "Lee Wiley 1952". Lee just set down in the woods, and gazed at the tree, the woods, and the sky. A few tears rolled down his cheeks, and he got a little choked up. He then got up and gazed at the sky. "Look how tall this tree has grown. I never would have imagined this tree still being here and so big. I think they left this one standing because of my carving, don't you, Chuck?" Lee stated as he admiringly looked on.

Standing there with his old time friends, they all headed back to the truck with a real good feeling inside. Chuck, walking with a cane, turned to Lee and said, "Look, Lee, I really thank you for inviting me to come along, and I just had some really good memories thinking about this." Barry said, "Let's stop and let Chuck rest. His leg is probably bothering him. Let's sit down on this big log."

"Hey, Lee, remember when we went swimming at "Logan's Rock". We really had a blast at that ole water hole, didn't we?" Chuck stated. "Lee, remember in Mr. Hill's class, when Barry put an Alka Seltzer in his mouth, and he started foaming?" "Yeah, Mr. Hill wouldn't get near him, because he thought he had rabies!" Lee laughed. They all started roaring. Barry added, "Then he started growling and acting like a rabid animal." Barry, Chuck, and Lee all started laughing so hard they couldn't stop. "Nothing like a good laugh," Barry proclaimed.

"I'll never forget our clubhouse," Lee reminisced. "I remember that, too," said Chuck, "Our moms baked a cake and put a dime wrapped in wax paper, and whoever got the dime wrapped in wax paper had to bring the next cake."

"Yeah, we couldn't wait to have another meeting, just to eat the cake," Bear announced. Finally our meetings only lasted a few months, because our mothers got tired of baking us a cake," said Bear.

After Lee got home, he decided to write about the old beech tree he wrote his name on. Lee had a talent for writing and expressing himself in words. He got up and retrieved a pencil and a pad and began scribbling. After a couple of hours, he had his article written. He decided to himself,"I think this article will be good for the Covey Friend, a weekly newspaper circulating in and around the town of Covey. His article went like this:

Man visits spot from youth and remembers times gone past

Truman was still president. The Korean War was going on. We lived on an old farm with dad share-cropping. This was a roaring coal mining town at the turn of the century.

Alec Jones ran the only store, a general store. He bought and sold mushrooms, gas, kerosene, groceries, dry goods and works. He had the biggest five cent sack of hard candy at Christmas around. I now know this was a little extra for us kids at Christmas. When the old "36" Chevy was on the blink, or had no tires, during the war, we would tie two burley sacks across the back of "Ole Bess" our mare and ride her to the store for groceries on the "bill". He knew dad and that we were good for the bill, and sometimes dad even walked and slid and pulled the sacks on the ice.

I remember we plowed gardens here in the spring; horses, walking plow, single section harrow, and old Rock Island wooden wheel box wagon to haul everything; $3 to $5 per garden. In winter I trapped rabbits (season was all winter long for me then). I sent away for American Garden seeds from Vippert Seed Co. I'd clean my rabbits real good, wrap them in wax paper, sack them and my seeds, hang them on the handlebars and take off pedaling for Streamtown. Was pretty cold riding, especially if you didn't have gloves or warm boots. The way you got there, I remember, was with one hand and warming the other in your coat pocket, and then change hands every other light pole. A country boy will survive you know.

A young boy will do a lot for that Red Ryder air rifle in that seed catalog, about worn out from looking and admiring it around a wood stove on cold winter nights. I got 25 cents out of my rabbits if I could, but would go to 15 cents, if I had to. I remember one cold day I stopped at, I think Grandma Beckley's and sold a few packs of seeds and had one rabbit left. She didn't want it, even at 15 cents, but finally took it for a dime. I think just to get rid of me. Anyhow that old coal stove really felt good and she had given me two fresh baked cookies and a glass of milk. Actually, I had quite a business going for me.

Well back to my story, I got off the school bus, grabbed my single barrel 12 gauge Stevens and headed for the woods. Had one old Hickory tree that most always got a fox squirrel out of, but it was too windy that night. I placed my shotgun against a small len tree, got out my jack knife and commenced carving my name and date in the smooth bark of a nearby beech tree. I carved it deep in the moist white wood and squared the edges and blew out the sawdust. Someday, but it will be a long, long time, I'll come back here, I said. After a few trips, about two weeks, I had my name etched and the date perfectly in the bark and wood of this tree.

Time went on—a family, kids, grandkids, death, sickness,

many good times, friends, hog roasts, fish frys, nice gardens, cars, trucks, tractors, boats, guns, pocket knifes, a few acres to pay taxes on, and I was caretaker for a few short years, trying to leave the place a little better for the next tenant.

Also several old hound dogs, most of them as sorry as I am. Just things we all endure as families and enjoy. Then suddenly, that old ball game we know as "life" is into the fourth and last quarter. Our goals then change, I think. I'm now retired and told my retired friends, John, Barry, and Chuck, if you want, it's time to go back to that ole beech tree. Getting permission, we left in the month of November. We stopped at the house; nobody was around, so we took the farm road back to the woods, past the same old barn we had many a corncob fight in.

The old double corn crib was still there, but moved to about where we had our garden. Dad plowed it with a walking plow and cultivated it with our mare "Bess" and a one horse five holt cultivator. Us kids rode and guided her, and she seldom stepped on a tomato or cabbage. We dragged hickory poles up to the wood pile with her and sawed them up in the saw back with the cross cut saw. We gathered walnuts in sacks on a mud sled; tied some together over her back and went to the house to hull them.

We drove back past the little creek and the old mine shaft and cinder pile, where the steam engines pulled the coal from the shaft and loaded in on railroad cars to Streamtown. I spent several hours in these woods looking for forked limbs for sling shots.

Relatives saved soft leather tongues of shoes and inner tubes for rock pouches for our sling shots. We caught our pumpkin seed sunfish and horned chubs in the little creek by the mine. We used our homemade bobbers and hooks from straight pins. Our bobbers we made from dry horse weeds.

Getting out of our truck, we walked across the old clay field toward the woods. Spent several cold weekends and Christmas vacations here shucking corn by hand with the horses, old box wagon with "knock" bank board on the back side. Everything had changed some, but finally found the old hickory tree. Found the len tree where I had leaned my shotgun; and there it was—the old beech tree. That long, long time has went pretty quick you know.

But heck, who else has sold a rabbit for a dime? Also to have received the gift of life, yet to be able to go back and see; where many years ago, I carved my name up on that tree.

Written by Lee Wiley

XXXV. Hopes and Dreams

Marly placed the card table in the middle of the living room floor. She sat the typewriter on the table. She commenced typing. She looked into space and her mind started wandering, and she thought, "Someday I will be an author, and I will be known for my novels and children's stories. Oh! That will be so great." Reminiscing of many memories, she wrote several poems. Being the country girl she was, Down in the Country was easy to write.

Down in the Country

Down in the country, that's the place to be,
Down in the country, that the place for me.
Strolling down a country road and over yonder,
A time to think, and a time to ponder.
A time to think, and quiet in the air,
A feeling of contentment everywhere.
The green, green grass in the spring.
To the familiar sounds of the birds with their ring.

In the summer in the heat of the day,
You can hear the children play.
The colorful autumn leaves in the fall,
The prettiest of all,
When the winter winds blow,
And covers everything with snow.
I'm a country girl and proud to be,
Down in the country, that's the place to be.

Marly loved the country. Walks down to the barn, watching the birds, the animals and nature were appalling, a beautiful sight to see. In the spring, the flowering shrubs and trees with their blooms, and the birds all chirping, and sounding as if they were singing melodies. The grape arbor was starting to sprout new leaves. The daffodils were in bloom. The smell of the blossoms of the cherry trees and other fruit trees were very aromatic. In the back yard the smell of the honeysuckle was spread throughout. The iris were in full bloom with beautiful colors.

Since Marly's aspiration was to be an author, she began writing poetry. She loved writing poetry. She wrote several and entered them into contests. She found an entry form for poetry contests in a magazine of her mothers. She entered her poems. Some of them became honorable mentions. One poem was published into a book. In this poem she wrote about taking time to enjoy the simple things in life. Taking and making time was priority. The poem went like this:

TAKE TIME

Take time,
Smile,
Take time,
Seek a friend,
Take time,
Be a friend,
Take time,
Slow down,
Take time,
Laugh, be joyful, and sing,
Take time,
Think,
Take time,
Be happy,
Take time,
Give thanks and pray.
In her next poems she wrote:

LOVE

Love is here to stay,
It will never go away,
Love for your family or a friend,
It all comes from within,
To cradle a child, or wipe a tear,
Give a hug to father or mother so dear,
To help an elderly lady across the street,
To give the neighbor kids an ice cream treat,
Love is the word,

The greatest thing I have ever heard,
Love, is here to stay,
and I hope it will never go away.

The one poem Marly wrote with herself in mind, was "My Secret Desire," and it went like this:

My secret desire is to become world-wide renown
For the contents of this poem,

For all nations, there shall be love, understanding, and peace,
Crime and terrorism shall cease.

The leaders, amicable and doing what's right,
No more wars, and no need to fight,

Leadership and stability,
Progress and capability.

Unity is the solution to the problems of today,
All for one, wholeness in every way.

If all this should come true,
just think of the goodness this would do.

Another poem she wrote that had so much meaning, and with all the modern technology in the future even more meaning. The poem went like this:

It's a Push-Button World

Sometimes I set, think, wonder, and struggle,
The complexities of the world, the universe,
So many questions unanswered,
Puzzles unsolved,
Unexplained phenomena,
It's a fascinating world,
It's a push-button world,
Modern technology,
Microscopic organisms,
Will the questions be answered?
Will the puzzles be solved?
Life goes on,
Time goes on,
Will the questions be answered?
Maybe....some day.

Marly sat out on the front porch and looked into the sky. With much thought she daydreamed, "I should write about my two favorite holidays, Thanksgiving and Christmas." She immediately ran inside and picked up her notepad, ran back out on the porch, sat in the swing, and started scribbling. The finished results were as follows:

THANKSGIVING

T is for the thanks of our many blessings
H is how the Mayflower landed on Plymouth Rock,
A is for the Almighty and his wondrous works,
N is for the necessities in life
K is for the kindness shown by our fellow man

S is for sincerity, honesty, and integrity,
G is for giving to the needy
I is for independence and freedom in our land
V is for the very most important thing: love
I is for incentive to be a better person
N is being a good neighbor
G is gathering together with our families and giving thanks

CHRISTMAS

C is for the Christ-child born in Bethlehem
H is for heaven, our eternal home above,
R is for the resurrection, when Jesus rose from the tomb,
I is for his innocence, when upon the cross
S is for Saviour, the one who died for us
T is for his teachings, recorded in the Bible
M is for the virgin Mary, the mother of Jesus,
A is for always, his ever abiding love,
S is the spiritual growth throughout that will unite the world.

After she finished these poems, she thought, "I need a couple more poems to sum up my thoughts, and she kept writing, "For the Beauty of the World."

FOR THE BEAUTY OF THE WORLD

God made the stars that shine so bright,
He divided day and night,
and there was light,
For the beauty of the world,
how amazing to me,

God made man and then woman,
to fulfill the earth and till the land,
How pretty, the mountains, the valleys,
rivers and seas,
the animals, flowers, and the trees,
O, how happy it makes me,
To see all the works of thee.

CHANGES IN LIFE

There are many changes in life,
Living means you have to accept them,
Sometimes accepting changes seems very hard,
With all the trials and tribulations,
Remember God is by your side,
Losing a loved one is a hard cross to bear,
Remember God has a plan for everything,
Keep your faith and he will guide you through,
Sometimes the road seems long and winding,
Hang in there, and keep believing in him.

A couple of other poems were inspired by her thoughts and imagination, which are as follows:

Writing Poetry

Here I sit, ready to write,
For each sentence there is a fight,

Trying to think of that special line,
It is very hard to find a rhyme,

In my mind, as I dwell,
I try to write very well,

All kinds of ideas go through my mind,
That one certain thought, I know I will find,

Thoughts go round and round,
Until I find that certain sound,

It gives me such a feeling of delight and pleasure,
And then I have my poem to treasure.

I WALK ALONE

When I walk alone, and look into the sky,
I wonder why o why,

Why do things happen the way they do?
Why do things happen to me and you?

Time never stands still,
And time never will,

There are always changes in life,
Amidst the toil and strife,

Fond memories are kept in the heart,
From them you will never part,

And when I walk alone, God will be my side,
And from him I will never hide.

Marly decided to start writing children's storybooks. She had great writing skills, and she knew how to get her words into easily interpreted stories. Many ideas came to her mind based on her own childhood and life experiences.

After all the struggles of the car wreck, everyday was beautiful. Marly had always seen the positive and couldn't wait for new things and new dreams. She could see herself writing a novel, and many children storybooks. She based her first storybooks about animal characters using the values and experiences she had growing up. Naming her characters was a lot of fun, and she felt her stories were witty, educational, but not didactic. Family started helping her with the names of the characters. Marly wanted to write children's books for the older child, also, with lots of ideas in mind.

She couldn't wait to attempt to write her novel, and the chances of an interview. Writing a novel would be a lot of research and work. "I know I can do it," Marly murmured to herself, "I have a lot of ideas and thoughts to write down. She would purchase a new tablet and start taking notes, lots and lots of notes, jotting down her different thoughts and ideas. "My new year's resolution is to start writing a novel and work and work until it is done," she murmured to herself.

Starting a novel was quite a challenge. Not just a short story, but a whole book. As she began, she edited and added and finally after five long years the book was looking and sounding more like a novel. Trying for perfection, Marly kept working and working, researching, and editing until finally the project was nearing completion.

XXXVI. A Journey Come True

Every morning Marly watched the Breakfast Hour on television. She, of course, would miss a few shows. The show was hosted by Cara Strebes and George Madden. The one thing that intrigued her the most was the interviews with the new authors. Her first thought was to finish her novel, and then to write a letter explaining her new experience of becoming an author. She also would write explaining that she had never been to New York, and would love to be a guest on the show. As she began her letter, she thought, "Oh, to be an author, to leave some information for my children and grandchildren, to let the whole world know, I am an author!"

She began commencing to write her letter, explaining in detail how she had written poems, and a few children's books, but her latest adventure was a novel. She knew everyone would love her writing. Quite confident she was of that! Her children's books were very educational. Every parent should know about the safety issues and learning issues she had written about. Confident she was! She was hoping to get an answer soon. Every day Marly went to the mail box, "I just know I will get an answer soon. Anyway, they can no more than say no. I know if you want to succeed, you just have to keep trying and never give up."

About three months later, she received a letter in the mail. The show host, George Madden, was inviting her to New York! She was so excited she almost fell off the chair. The one thing she had dreamed and hoped for was coming true. "Just think, George Madden is going to interview me. I must buy a couple of new outfits. I have to look my best. Maybe I will purchase some new make up. I can't wait," she thought. "Heavenly days! Marly, your dream is coming true," Sarah boasted, "I knew in my heart this day was coming for you."

Seth spoke up after he began putting his pipe out, "Well, I'll be, I have an author for a daughter, A pretty one at that! I'll have to tell all my friends about this. You're going to be the second interview, right?" Complimenting his children and bragging about them was a natural thing for him. "That's right, dad," Marly responded, "and I am so excited."

As Marly packed her luggage, Sarah kept giving her tips. "Now keep your posture straight. Seth and Sarah always stressed good posture. Pull your shoulders back," Sarah coaxed. Seth and Sarah drove Marly to the Tidville Airport just outside of Covey to board the commuter plane. They watched her enter the small airport, and said their good-byes.

"You be careful, Marly, and remember mom and dad loves you!"

On the trip to the airport, Seth had kept telling her to eat regular meals and not upset her system. He was such a health nut, he knew Marly could get her system out of whack.

Marly first boarded the commuter plane to get to the main airport. Just being a little nervous and edgy, the businessman in front of her noticed she was a little frightened. He said, "Been on a flight before, ma'am?" "This is my first flight," Marly hastily replied. "Ah, it's a piece of cake," he stated. After that things just fell in place. The flight was a piece of cake.

The commuter plane landed a beautiful landing. Marly was contemplating how to find the right gate, and hurry to the right exit and then she would be on her way to New York. The businessman spoke again, "You can just follow me. I have enough time, and I am going in the same direction. I will show you."

"That will be great," Marly responded. Off they went, and as the businessman left, he said, "Good luck with your book and interview!" Marly had told him of her venture. "Gee, thanks, for assisting me to the right gate!" Marly expressed. She thought, "How helpful he was! I didn't even get his name. I'll just think of him as an angel that helped me."

She was on a plane to New York. Her dream was finally coming true. Sitting on the large comfy seats right next to a window, Marly thought, "On a plane, bus, or ship you can go anywhere, flying in the sky, above the billowy clouds so high, thinking of all the things she could do." Marly got out her pad and pencil, and she thought, "I may jot down a few notes, if anything comes to mind." Thinking of her childhood and her good memories, she wrote: There is no other than your mother. This will be a good poem, and I will have to write down some verses," she thought. She soon drifted to sleep.

As Marly woke up, the stewardess was announcing to restrain from removing your seat belts, the landing will be a little bumpy as we have some turmoil in the weather. "That's a scary thought," muttered Marly, "How exciting we were landing in New York City and I had slept the whole trip!" Sitting by the window she thought she could view the terrain. Maybe she could on the way home. Finally the stewardess announced, "Please take your seat belts off, and starting with the first aisle, you can move from your seats, exit the plane, and head on to your destinations."

Exiting the plane, Marly walked down the steps onto the walkway. Heading for a cab, she looked up and all she could see was the beautiful blue sky and lots of skyscrapers. The sky was dotted with little marshmallow clouds. The clouds were so billowy and fluffy amongst the tall buildings.

Instead of a cab, she was greeted by the chauffeur. My name is Ted Byer, your chauffeur. I will collect your luggage, and transport you to the plush hotel, "The Hilton", and I hope you enjoy your trip. The limousine is waiting for you."

"What! a limousine, Wow! I guess I wasn't expecting this," she enthusiastically commented. "Oh, my goodness! The buildings are so tall and large. Wow! Oh, My gosh, look over there!" she said to Ted. "Is that where I will be going?" she gestured. "What is going to happen next?" she dreamingly thought as she picked up her handbag and magazine as they entered the limousine. Ted dropped Marly off at the Hilton. The porter helped her with the luggage. She went to the front desk and retrieved her key and headed to the fourth floor, room 465.

The next morning she rose, showered, and turned the television on. Just catching up on the news and the weather, she sat in her comfy chair in amazement the time had arrived. Finally her dream had come true. The knock on the door caught her attention. The room service had delivered her breakfast and a memo. She looked over her memo she had received. The memo stated she had an appointment to the beauty shop on the fifth floor, room 561, and a complete make-over to get ready for the show.

Marly picked up the phone, retrieved the outside line, and dialed her parents. "Mom I was not expecting all of this! I get my hair styled, a pedicure and manicure, and also a facial. I have a make-up consultant after that! Can you believe all this!" she shrieked. Sarah repeated and began rambling on to Seth and catching him up on the news. Her parents were so proud, and she was so excited. Sarah was telling all her friends. Seth was bragging about her interview to his friends and relatives, "I knew Marly was a great author, and now everyone will know. Be sure to turn your t.v. on Friday morning for the show to be aired at nine o'clock sharp. She is the second guest."

The fifth floor was her next destination for the complete makeover. The fifth floor was also the beauty shop. Eating slowly and enjoying her breakfast and coffee, she realized the interview was just a few hours away. Marly headed out the door, to the stairs and up to the fifth floor. "You must be Marly Wiley," Vanessa spoke as she opened the door, "We were expecting you."

"Make yourself at home with a magazine, and we will be with you next," Vanessa softly spoke. The Breakfast Hour started early, so she would have to be done in a couple of hours. Going through all the makeover ritual was quite exciting, something Marly had always wanted to do.

XXXVII. The Big Interview

After getting all finished, she headed back down to her room. She donned her new black suit with a red blouse and scarf and earrings and necklace to match. She felt like she was on cloud nine. "What a great feeling!" she thought to herself. Next the limousine was waiting for her to arrive at the Breakfast Hour guest room.

She walked in and entered the room, and was greeted by the host, Steve Madden. "Hi, you must be Marly, I am Steve Madden and I will be interviewing you. Just make yourself at home, sit down and relax until we call your name. Good luck on your interview," he warmly suggested. "Thank you, Steve. I am glad to meet you and I can't wait till the interview," Marly excitedly announced.

As she waited, the cameras were rolling, the director announcing the interviews and the different segments for the show. "Just wave and smile, as we come around and film you, Marly," the stagehand suggested, "The camera will be on you a short time. Oh, now here they come." She looked up, smiled and waved her hand.

Shortly later she heard the host, Steve Madden, announce, "I would like to introduce our next guest today, Marly Wiley. She is an author. She has written a few poems, some children's stories, and her latest adventure, a novel, "Imaginary Minds." We are going to interview her, and we will talk about her novel.

Marly walked out with great poise. She was looking forward to her first interview. "Hi Marly, we are glad to meet you. This is Cara Strebes, my co-host and I am Steve Madden," Steve spoke. "I am glad to meet you and thanks for inviting me to your show," Marly replied. Of course, no one knew her body was shaking and she had goose bumps. "From reading the introductory to your book, I see you are a country girl and grew up on a farm from a small town in Indiana. We read your novel and we would like to ask you how and what derived you to write your novel?" Cara asked, "Also I want you to know your book held my interest throughout the whole book. What a book!"

As Marly began speaking, she became very comfortable and as if this was really her time to shine. "I thought about my childhood, and I realized I had a lot to write about. Growing up in the country, the times were so different than the youth growing up these days, that I thought I should document some of the different events that happened and write a book so others could see just exactly how growing up in those years were like; I added a few different chapters to keep the interest growing," Marly responded, "Of course, a few of the episodes did not actually happen, but this was the fun part of the book. I could write with my own imagination, as the title implies. One of my best friends, Pat Flynn, said, "Marly, did you know, I think everyone has a book in them, if they would just jot it down." I thought, "How true!"

"Did your brothers really do everything you say in the book?" Steve inquired. "Yes, these stories were true. My oldest brother was always speaking of the different stories, and this is when I realized the time to write a book had come," Marly mentioned, "I hope the readers can enjoy reading the book and some of the older people may relate to the times. Most of the younger ones can only imagine."

"I can only imagine hearing them speak of their times, and the laughter amongst you all," Steve said. "Yes, we had some good reminiscing times. When I told my oldest brother about my novel, he would say, "Did you put this in, etc.?" I am sending members of my family a copy, and I imagine there might be a few tears," Marly added.

"Did you ever think about your book being filmed for a movie?" Steve questioned. "Yes, as I was flying and in the plane, I started dreaming. You know dreams can come true. What if this book becomes a movie? Who will the star be? I guess this was a great thought. I do have some actors and actresses in mind, but I guess we will just have to wait and see. This is much too early to mention any stars," Marly informed.

"You spoke of a car wreck. Did you ever think you might not recover enough to walk?" Cara asked. "Right after the car wreck, this constantly crossed my mind. Do you know how happy I am that I can walk and I did recover? For nine long months, I watched others moving around and doing everything they wanted. Sitting back, and hoping some day you can walk again, was hard to take. I sat back, and told myself that my situation could be a lot worse. I was able to mend, and thank goodness for that. After this, I felt like I could conquer the world, if you know what I mean. This chapter was so hard to write, because this brought back lots of memories. I always regretted the hardships that I brought to my parents. We all conquered the rough times, and I feel like I am a stronger person because of this. I never take anything for granted ever. I appreciate every day that I have," Marly went on to explain. My parents are home waiting with anxiety wondering what all is happening. After I get back to my hotel, I will call and update them of my whole journey, which has been awesome!

"Economics were hard, and being scarce with food and gas during those times. Do you remember how this was?" Steve asked. "I was much younger, but I remember my mother telling me of the hardships," Marly informed, "My parents were hard workers and they were always able to provide. We were much more fortunate than many of our neighbors, and also, we had a lot of love in our family, and all the money in the world can't take the place of a happy, loving home.

"There were a few stories in your book, I am assuming, never really happened. Am I right?" Steve questioned. "Yes, a couple of the stories added interest to the plot, but most were based around experiences I had during the time I grew up," Marly went on to explain. "I also loved your poetry, and I hear you want to write more children's books. What led you to write children's stories and will you write more poetry?" Cara inquired.

"My strongest desire is to write more children's books. I have two or three I am winding up. They are geared toward the older child, about six to ten. I started my first two books with pre-school to second grade in mind. I used animal characters to lead the story. I plan on writing a little differently for the older age. I can't wait to finish them up.

"Thanks for being with us today, Marly. I wonder if we could have you back when you wind up those children's books and any more novels you might write, and we will talk about your newest projects. Please let us know, so you can come back and we will have your second interview," Steve offered.

Marly rose from her seat, shook their hands, and just like her dad, she said, “You bet, and thanks so much for having me. This is an experience I will never forget. Thanks again,” Marly motioned and waved her hand at the audience as she exited the room.